INTO
THE *Dreaming*

Into the Dreaming

Karen Marie Moning

DELACORTE PRESS | NEW YORK

Published in the United States by Delacorte Press, an imprint of The Random House Publishing Group, a division of Random House, Inc., New York.

DELACORTE PRESS is a registered trademark of Random House, Inc., and the colophon is a trademark of Random House, Inc.

ISBN: 978-0-345-53522-1
eBook ISBN: 978-0-345-53523-8

Printed in the United States of America on acid-free paper

www.bantamdell.com

2 4 6 8 9 7 5 3 1

FIRST DELACORTE PRESS EDITION

Book design by Casey Hampton

MAY 16 2012

*For my sister Laura, whose talent for shaping unformed clay extends
to far more than that which can be fired in a kiln.*

*May your gardens ever bloom in lush profusion,
may your peach jam and pecan chicken always taste like heaven,
may the artistry inside your soul always find expression,
and may you always know how loved you are.*

FOREWORD

IF YOU'VE PICKED UP THIS BOOK THAT MEANS YOU'RE ONE OF four things: a fan of my Highlander series, a fan of my Fever books, neither, or both.

If you're one of my Highlander fans, this book is for you. Written between *Kiss of the Highlander* and *The Dark Highlander, Into the Dreaming* is pure romance, with the first, faint strains of a darker music: a glimpse into the world of the icy, inhuman Seelie and Unseelie courts that I eventually developed into my Fever series.

If you're a Fever fan and haven't read my Highlander books, this is where it all began, when I first knew there was another, much darker story waiting to be told. Many of you have written to ask me how the Faery World in *Into the Dreaming* fits chronologically into the Fever series and the answer is: not at all. What happens in *Into the Dreaming* didn't happen in the Fever world. It's completely separate, although obviously the outline of the Fae characters/court and the themes are the same. Think of this novella as the seeds of an idea I couldn't write yet, so I made sketchy notes then went back to my day job, writing romance novels until the time was right. Or rather until I woke up one morning from a long and very detailed dream to find the story as unavoidable as a ten-car pileup in heavy fog on a one-lane road in a dark tunnel.

If you're a fan of both series, good to see you again! There are extras from both worlds included in this compilation. You'll find a book proposal for an unwritten story, *Ghost of a Chance,* deleted scenes from *Kiss of the Highlander,* and a good chunk of *The Dark Highlander Lite,* the version that didn't get published, plus a bit about what was going on in my world at the time.

You'll also find a sneak peek at my new graphic novel *Fever Moon: The Fear Dorcha,* a 150-plus-page, full-color hardcover, which features Mac & Barrons in an all-new original adventure that takes place during *Shadowfever.* For those of you who are new to my Fever series, we've included a preview of those books as well.

If you've never read either series and picked up this book solely on the cover and blurb, welcome! This collection will give you a look at the worlds I write about, and is a great way to dip your toe in and see if you like the water.

Special thanks to Random House for getting *Into the Dreaming* back out there in a wonderful package. It had gone out of print and many readers either couldn't find it or told me they'd paid ridiculous amounts for a dog-eared paperback copy.

A tongue-in-cheek, sexy romp, *Into the Dreaming* was in-
spired by my sisters: Laura with her fabulous cooking, and
Elizabeth with her infamous Silly Jane jokes. Jane Sillee
(could I be more obvious?) thinks if you toss stellar sex into
that mix, you've got all you need for a wonderful life. I'm
inclined to agree.

Drop by my Facebook page or website message board
after you've finished. I love to hear from readers!

Stay to the lights,

Karen

CONTENTS

INTO THE Dreaming

His hard, wet body glistened in the moonlight as he emerged from the ocean. Brilliant eyes of stormy aquamarine met hers, and her heart raced.

He stood naked before her, the look in his eyes offering everything, promising eternity.

When he cupped one strong hand at the nape of her neck and drew her closer to receive his kiss, her lips parted on a sigh of dreamy anticipation.

His kiss was at first gentle, then as stormy as the man himself, for he was a man of deep secrets, a man of deeper passion, her Highlander.

One hand became two buried in her hair, one kiss became a second of fierce and fiery desire, then he swept her into his arms, raced up the castle steps, and carried her to his bedchamber . . .

—From the unpublished manuscript
Highland Fire by Jane Sillee

One

928

NOT QUITE SCOTLAND

It was a land of shadows and ice.

Of gray. And grayer. And black.

Deep in the shadows lurked inhuman creatures, twisted of limb and hideous of countenance. Things one did well to avoid seeing.

Should the creatures enter the pale bars of what passed for light in the terrible place, they would die, painfully and slowly. As would he—the mortal Highlander imprisoned within columns of sickly light—should he succeed in breaking the chains that held him and seek escape through those terrifying shadows.

Jagged cliffs of ice towered above him. A frigid wind shrieked through dark labyrinthine canyons, bearing a susurrus of desolate voices and faint, hellish screams. No sun, no fair breeze of Scotland, no scent of heather penetrated his frozen, bleak hell.

6

He hated it. His very soul cringed at the horror of the place.

He ached for the warmth of the sun on his face and hungered for the sweet crush of grass beneath his boots. He would have given years of his life for the surety of his stallion between his thighs and the solid weight of his claymore in his grip.

He dreamed—when he managed to escape the agony of his surroundings by retreating deep into his mind—of the blaze of a peat fire, scattered with sheaves of heather. Of a woman's warm, loving caresses. Of buttery, golden-crusted bread hot from the hearth. Simple things. Impossible things.

For the son of a Highland chieftain, who'd passed a score and ten in resplendent mountains and vales, five years was an intolerable sentence; an incarceration that would be withstood only by force of will, by careful nurturing of the light of hope within his heart.

But he was a strong man, with the royal blood of Scottish kings running hot and true in his veins. He would survive. He would return and reclaim his rightful place, woo and win a bonny lass with a tender heart and a tempestuous spirit like his mother, and fill the halls of Dun Haakon with the music of wee ones.

With such dreams, he withstood five years in the hellish wasteland.

Only to discover the dark king had deceived him.

His sentence had never been five years at all, but five *faery* years: five hundred years in the land of shadow and ice.

On that day when his heart turned to ice within his breast, on that day when a single tear froze upon his cheek, on that day when he was denied even the simple solace of dreaming, he came to find his prison a place of beauty.

"My queen, the Unseelie king holds a mortal captive."

The Seelie queen's face remained impassive, lest her court see how deeply disturbing she found the messenger's news. Long had the Seelie Court of Light and the Unseelie Court of Dark battled. Long had the Unseelie king provoked her. "Who is this mortal?" she asked coolly.

"Aedan MacKinnon, son and heir of the Norse princess Saucy Mary and Findanus MacKinnon, from Dun Haakon on the Isle of Skye."

"Descendent of the Scottish king, Kenneth McAlpin," the queen mused aloud. "The Unseelie king grows greedy, his aim lofty, if he seeks to turn the seed of the McAlpin to his dark ways. What bargain did he strike with this mortal?"

"He sent his current Hand of Vengeance into the world to bring death to the mortal's clansmen yet bartered that if the mortal willingly consented to spend five years in his kingdom, he would spare his kin."

"And the MacKinnon agreed?"

"The king concealed from him that five years in Faery is five centuries. Still, as grandseed of the McAlpin, I suspect the MacKinnon would have accepted the full term to protect his clan."

"What concession does the king make?" the queen asked shrewdly. Any bargain between faery and mortal must hold the possibility for the human to regain his freedom. Still, no mortal had ever bested a faery in such a bargain.

"At the end of his sentence, he will be granted one full

8

cycle of the moon in the mortal world, at his home at Dun Haakon. If, by the end of that time, he is loved and loves in return, he will be free. If not, he serves as the king's new Hand of Vengeance until the king chooses to replace him, at which time he dies."

The queen made a sound curiously like a sigh. By such cruel methods had the Unseelie king long fashioned his deadly, prized assassin—his beloved Vengeance—by capturing a mortal, driving him past human limits into madness, indurating him to all emotion, then endowing him with special powers and arts.

Since the Unseelie king was barred entrance to the human world, he trained his Vengeance to carry out his orders, to hold no act too heinous. Mortals dared not even whisper the icy assassin's name, lest they inadvertently draw his merciless attention. If a man angered the Unseelie king, Vengeance punished the mortal's clan, sparing no innocents. If grumblings about the faery were heard, Vengeance silenced them in cruelly imaginative ways. If the royal house was not amenable to the faery world, Vengeance toppled kings as carelessly as one might sweep a chessboard.

Until now, it had been the Unseelie king's wont to abduct an insignificant mortal, one without clan who would not be missed, to train as his Vengeance. He went too far this time, the Seelie queen brooded, abducting a blood grandson of one of fair Scotia's greatest kings—a man of great honor, noble and true of heart.

She would win this mortal back.

The queen was silent for a time. Then, "Ah, what five hundred years in that place will do to him," she breathed in a

chilling voice. The Unseelie king had named the terms of his
bargain well. Aedan MacKinnon would still be mortal at the
end of his captivity but no longer remotely human when released. Once, long ago and never forgotten, she'd traversed
that forbidden land herself, danced upon a pinnacle of black
ice, slept within the dark king's velvet embrace . . .

"Perhaps an enchanted tapestry," she mused, "to bring the
MacKinnon the one true mate to his heart." She could not
fight the Unseelie king directly, lest the clash of their magic
too gravely damage the land. But she could and would do all
in her power to ensure Aedan MacKinnon found love at the
end of his imprisonment.

"My queen," the messenger offered hesitantly, "they shall
have but one bridge of the moon in the sky. Perhaps they
should meet in the Dreaming."

The queen pondered a moment. The Dreaming: that elusive, much-sought, everforgotten realm where mortals occa-
sionally brushed pale shoulder to iridescent wing with the
fairy. That place where mortals would be astonished to know
battles were won and lost, universes born, and true love pre-
ordained, from Cleopatra and Mark Antony to Abelard and
Heloise. The lovers could meet in the Dreaming and share a
lifetime of loving before they ever met in the mortal realm. It
would lay a grand foundation for success of her plan.

"Wisely spoken," the queen agreed. Rising from her floral
bower with fluid grace, she raised her arms and began to sing.

From her melody a tapestry was woven, of faery lore, of
bits of blood and bone, of silken hair from the great, great-
grandson of the McAlpin, of ancient rites known only to the
True Race. As she sang, her court chanted:

Into the Dreaming lure them deep
where they shall love whilst they doth sleep
then in the waking both shall dwell
'til love's fire doth melt his ice-borne hell.

And when the tapestry was complete, the queen marveled.

"Is this truly the likeness of Aedan MacKinnon?" she asked, eyeing the tapestry with unmistakable erotic interest.

"I have seen him, and it is so," the messenger replied, wetting his lips, his gaze fixed upon the tapestry.

"Fortunate woman," the queen said silkily.

The faery queen went to him in the Dreaming, well into his sentence, when he was quite mad. Tracing a curved nail against his icy jaw, she whispered in his ear, "Hold fast, MacKinnon, for I have found you the mate to your soul. She will warm you. She will love you above all others."

The monster chained to the ice threw back his dark head and laughed.

It was not a human sound at all.

Two

PRESENT DAY
OLDENBURG, INDIANA

JANE SILLEE HAD AN INTENSELY PASSIONATE RELA-
tionship with her postman.

It was classic love-hate.

The moment she heard him whistling his way down her
walk, her heart kicked into overtime, a sappy smile curved
her lips, and her breathing quickened.

But the moment he failed to deliver the acceptance letter
extolling the wonders of her manuscript, or worse, handed
her a rejection letter, she hated him. *Hated* him. Knew it was
his fault somehow. That maybe, just maybe, a publisher had
written glowing things about her, he'd dropped the letter because he was careless, the wind had picked it up and carried
it off, and even now her bright and shining future lay sodden
and decomposing in a mud puddle somewhere.

Just how much could a federal employee be trusted, anyway?
she brooded suspiciously. He could be part of some covert

12

study designed to determine how much one tortured writer could endure before snapping and turning into a pen-wielding felon.

"Purple prose, my ass," she muttered, balling up the latest rejection letter. "I only used black ink. I can't *afford* a color ink cartridge." She kicked the door of her tiny apartment shut and slumped into her secondhand Naugahyde recliner.

Massaging her temples, she scowled. She simply had to get this story published. She'd become convinced it was the only way she was ever going to get him out of her mind.

Him. Her sexy, dark-haired Highlander. The one who came to her in dreams.

She was hopelessly and utterly in love with him.

And at twenty-four, she was really beginning to worry about herself.

Sighing, she unballed and smoothed the rejection letter. This one was the worst of the lot and got pretty darned personal, detailing numerous reasons why her work was incompetent, unacceptable, and downright idiotic. "But I *do* hear celestial music when he kisses me," Jane protested. "At least in my dreams I do," she muttered.

Crumpling it again, she flung it across the room and closed her eyes.

Last night she'd danced with him, her perfect lover.

They'd waltzed in a woodland clearing, caressed by a fragrant forest breeze, beneath a black velvet canopy of glittering stars. She'd worn a gown of shimmering lemon-colored silk. He'd worn a plaid of crimson and black atop a soft, laced, linen shirt. His gaze had been so tender, so passionate, his hands so strong and masterful, his tongue so hot and hungry and—

Jane opened her eyes, sighing gustily. How was she supposed to have a normal life when she'd been dreaming about the man since she was old enough to remember dreaming? As a child, she'd thought him her guardian angel. But as she'd ripened into a young woman, he'd become so much more.

In her dreams, they'd skipped the dance of the swords between twin fires at Beltane atop a majestic mountain while sipping honeyed mead from pewter tankards. How could a cheesy high-school prom replete with silver disco ball suspended from the ceiling accompanied by plastic cups of Hawaiian Punch compare to that?

In her dreams, he'd deftly and with aching gentleness removed her virginity. Who wanted a Monday-night-football-watching, beer-drinking, insurance adjuster/frustrated wannabe-pro-golfer?

In her dreams he'd made love to her again and again, his heated touch shattering her innocence and awakening her to every manner of sensual pleasure. And although in her waking hours, she'd endeavored to lead a normal life, to fall for a flesh-and-blood man, quite simply, no mere man could live up to her dreams.

"You're hopeless. Get over him, already," Jane muttered to herself. If she had a dollar for every time she'd told herself that, she'd own Trump Tower. And the air rights above it.

Glancing at the clock, she pushed herself up from the chair. She was due at her job at the Smiling Cobra Café in

14

twenty minutes, and if she was late again, Laura might make good on her threat to fire her. Jane had a tendency to forget the time, immersed in her writing or research or just plain daydreaming.

You're a throwback to some other era, Jane, Laura had said a dozen times.

And indeed, Jane had always felt she'd been born in the wrong century. She didn't own a car and didn't want one. She hated loud noises, condos, and skyscrapers and loved the unspoiled countryside and cozy cottages. She suffered living in an apartment because she couldn't afford a house. Yet.

She wanted her own vegetable garden and fruit orchard. Maybe a milking cow to make butter and cheese and fresh whipped cream. She longed to have babies—three boys and three girls would do nicely.

Yes, in this day and age, she was definitely a throwback. To caveman days, probably, she thought forlornly. When her girlfriends had graduated from college and rushed off with their business degrees and briefcases to work in steel-and-glass high-rises, determined to balance career, children, and marriage, Jane had taken her BA in English and gone to work in a coffee shop, harboring simpler aspirations. All she wanted was a low-pressure job that wouldn't interfere with her writing ambitions. Jane figured the skyrocketing divorce rate had a whole lot to do with people trying to tackle too much. Being a wife, lover, best friend, and mother seemed like a pretty full plate to her. And if—no, she amended firmly—*when* she finally got published, writing romance would be a perfect at-home career. She'd have the best of both worlds.

Right, and someday my prince will come . . .

Shrugging off an all-too-familiar flash of depression, she wheeled her bike out of the tiny hallway between the kitchen and bedroom and grabbed a jacket and her backpack. As she opened the door she glanced back over her shoulder to be sure she'd turned off her computer and ran smack into the large package that had been left on her doorstep.

That hadn't been there half an hour ago when she'd plucked her mail from the sweaty, untrustworthy hands of the postman. Perhaps he'd returned with it, she mused; it *was* large. It must be her recent Internet order from the online used bookstore, she decided. It was earlier than she'd anticipated, but she wasn't complaining.

She'd be blissfully immersed in larger-than-life heroes, steamy romance, and alternate universes for the next few days. Glancing at her watch again, she sighed, propped her bike against the doorjamb, dragged the box into her apartment, wheeled her bike back out into the hall, then shut and locked the door. She knew better than to open the box now. She'd quickly progress from stealing a quick glance at the covers, to opening a book, to getting completely lost in a fantasy world.

And then Laura would fire her for sure.

It was nearly one in the morning by the time Jane finally got home. If she'd had to make one more extra-shot, one-half decaf, Venti, double-cup, two-Sweet'n-Low, skim with light foam latte for one more picky, anorexic bimbo, she might have done bodily harm to a customer. Why couldn't anyone drink good old-fashioned coffee anymore? Heavy on the sugar—*loads* of cream. Life was too short to count calories. At least that's what she told herself each time the scale snidely

16

deemed her plump for five foot three and three-quarter inches.

With a mental shrug, she scattered thoughts of work from her mind. It was over. She'd done her time, and now she was free to be just Jane. And she couldn't wait to start that new vampire romance she'd been dying to read!

After brushing her teeth, she slipped out of her jeans and sweater and into her favorite nightie, the frilly, romantic one with tiny daisies and cornflowers embroidered at the scooped neckline. She tugged the box near her bed before dropping cross-legged on the stuffed, old-fashioned feather ticks. Slicing the packing-tape seal with a metal nail file, she paused and sniffed, as an irresistibly spicy scent wafted from the box. Jasmine, sandalwood, and something else . . . something elusive that nudged her past feeling dreamily romantic to positively aroused. *Great time to read a romance,* she thought ruefully, *with no man to attack when the love scenes heat up.* Untouched except in her dreams, her hormones tended to simmer at a constant gentle boil.

With a wry smile, she dug past the purple Styrofoam peanuts and paused again when her hands closed on rough fabric. Frowning, she tugged it free, sending peanuts skittering across the hardwood floor. The exotic scent filled the room, and she glanced at the closed casement window, bemused by the sudden sultry breeze that lifted strands of her curly red hair and pressed her nightie close to her body.

Perplexed, she placed the folded fabric on her bed, then checked the box. No postmark, no return address, but her name was printed on the top in large block letters, next to her apartment number.

"Well, I'm not paying for it," she announced, certain a hefty bill would shortly follow. "I didn't order it." Darned if she was paying for something she didn't want. She had a hard enough time affording the things she did want.

Irritated that she had no new books to read, she plucked idly at the fabric, then unfolded it and spread it out on the bed.

And sat motionless, her mouth ajar.

"This is *not* funny," she breathed, shocked. "No," she amended in a shaky whisper, "this is not *possible*."

It was a tapestry, exquisitely woven of brilliant colors, featuring a magnificent Highland warrior standing before a medieval castle, legs spread in an arrogant stance that clearly proclaimed him master of the keep. Clad in a crimson and black tartan, adorned with clan regalia, both his hands were extended as if reaching for her.

And it was *him*. Her dream man.

Taking a deep breath, she closed her eyes, then opened them slowly.

It was still him. Each detail precisely as she'd dreamed him, from his powerful forearms and oh-so-capable hands to his luminous aqua eyes, to his silky dark hair and his sensual mouth.

How she would have loved living in medieval times, with a man like him!

Beneath his likeness, carefully stitched, was his name. "Aedan MacKinnon," she whispered.

Mortals did not bide captivity in Faery well—they did not age and time stretched into infinity—and Aedan MacKinnon was no exception. It took a mere two hundred years of being imprisoned in ice, coupled with the king's imaginative tortures, for the Highlander to forget who he'd once been. The king devoted the next two centuries to brutally training and conditioning him.

He educated the Highlander in every language spoken and instructed him in the skills, customs, and mores of each century so that he might move among mankind in any era without arousing suspicion. He trained him in every conceivable weapon and manner of fighting and endowed him with special gifts.

During the fifth and final century, the king dispatched him frequently to the mortal realm to dole out one punishment or another. Eradicating the mortal's confounded sense of honor had proven impossible, so the king utilized dark spells to compel his obedience during such missions, and if the conflict caused the mortal immeasurable pain, the king cared not. Only the end result interested the Unseelie king.

After five centuries, the man who'd once been known as Aedan MacKinnon had no recollection of his short span of thirty years in the mortal realm long ago. He no longer knew that he was mortal himself and did not understand why his king was banishing him there now.

But the king knew he owned his Vengeance only once he had fulfilled all the terms of the original agreement—the agreement the Highlander had long ago forgotten. In accordance with that agreement, the king was forbidden to coerce him with magic or instruction of any kind: Vengeance was to have his month at Dun Haakon, free of the king's meddling.

Still, the king could offer a few suggestions . . . suggestions he knew his well-trained Vengeance would construe as direct orders. After informing Vengeance—to whom time had little meaning—that the year was 1428, refreshing his knowledge of the proper customs of the century, and giving him a weighty pouch of gold coin, the Unseelie king "suggested," choosing his words carefully:

"Your body will have needs in the mortal realm. You must eat, but I would suggest you seek only bland foods."

"As you will it, my liege," Vengeance replied.

"The village of Kyleakin is near the castle wherein you'll reside. It might be best that you go there only to procure supplies and not dally therein."

"As you will it, my liege."

"Above all else, it would be unwise to seek the company of female humans or permit them to touch you."

"As you will it, my liege." A weighty pause, then, "Must I leave you?"

"It is for but a short time, my Vengeance."

Vengeance took a final look at the land he found so beautiful. "As you will it, my liege," he said.

Jane studied the tapestry, running her fingers over it, touching his face, wondering why she'd never thought to try to create a likeness of him before. What a joy it was to gaze upon him in her waking hours! She wondered where it had come from, why it had been delivered to her, if it meant he *really* existed out there somewhere. Perhaps, she decided, he'd lived long ago, and this tapestry had been his portrait, handed down from generation to generation. It looked as if it had been lovingly cared for over the centuries.

Still, that didn't explain how or why it had been sent to

her. She'd never told anyone about the strange recurring dreams of her Highlander. There was no logical explanation for the tapestry's arrival. Baffled, she shook her head, scattering the troubling questions from her mind, and gazed longingly at his likeness.

Funny, she mused, she'd been dreaming about him for forever, but until now she had never known his last name. He'd been only Aedan and she only Jane.

Their dream nights had been void of small talk. Theirs had been a wordless love—the quietly joyous joining of two halves of a whole. No need for questions, only for the dancing and the loving and, one day not too far off, babies. Their love transcended the need for language. The language of the heart was unmistakable.

Aedan MacKinnon. She rolled the name over and over in her mind.

She wondered and wished and ached for him, until at last, she rested her cheek against his face, curled up, and tenderly kissed his likeness. As she drifted into dreams—in that peculiar moment preceding deep sleep that always felt to Jane like falling—she thought she heard a silvery voice softly singing. The words chimed clearly, echoing in her mind:

> *Free him from his ice-borne hell*
> *And in his century you both may dwell.*
> *In the Dreaming hast thou loved him*
> *Now, in the Waking must thou save him.*

And then she thought no more, swept away on a tide of dreams.

Three

WHEN JANE AWAKENED THERE WAS A KITTEN DRAPED ACROSS her neck, napping. Paws buried in her curly hair, it kneaded and purred deliriously, its tiny body thrumming with pleasure.

She blinked, trying to wake up. *Had there been a kitten in the box, too?* she wondered, petting its silky belly, feeling terribly guilty for failing to notice it earlier. How had it breathed in the box? Poor thing must be starved! She thought she might have some tuna in the pantry to give the little tyke. Stretching gingerly, she lifted the tiny creature off her neck and rolled over onto her side.

And shrieked.

"L-L-*Lake!*" she sputtered. "There's a lake in my bedroom!" Three feet away from her. Deep blue and gently lapping at the shore. The shore that she'd been sleeping on.

Stunned, she sat up, performing a frantic mental check.

Bedroom, gone. Apartment, gone. Tapestry, gone. Kitten, here. Nightie—

Gone.

"I am *so* not in the mood for an inadequacy dream," Jane hissed.

Purple flowery stuff. Here. Castle. Here.

Castle?

She rubbed her eyes with the heels of her palms. The kitten mewed and gave her an insistent head-butt, demanding more belly rubbing. She clutched the tiger-striped kitten and gaped at the castle. It looked very much like the castle she visited in her dreams, except this castle was in near ruin; a mere quarter of it stood undamaged.

"I'm still sleeping," she whispered. "I'm just dreaming that I woke up, right?" She would have been only mildly surprised had the kitten bared pearly teeth and cheekily replied.

But it didn't, so, cradling its tiny body, she rose and started walking toward the castle, wincing as her bare feet padded across stones. She tried to imagine herself some dream clothes and shoes, but it didn't work. *So much for controlling one's subconscious,* she thought. As she gazed at the portion of the castle still intact—a square central tower abutted by one wing that sported a smaller round tower—her gaze was caught by a dark flutter atop the walls. As she watched, the flutter became a shirt, the shirt a shoulder, the shoulder a man.

Her man.

She stood motionless, gazing up.

Vengeance could not fathom what had driven him to climb to the top of the tower. He'd intended to sit in the hall of the strange castle, eating only enough to survive, gazing at nothing, waiting to return to his king, but moments ago he'd felt an overwhelming compulsion to go outside. Being outside, however, was disconcerting—no cool shadows and ice but riotous color and heat—so he'd climbed instead to the walk atop the tower, where he felt less besieged by the foreign landscape.

And there she stood—the lass.

Bare as she'd been fashioned.

Something low in his gut twisted. Mayhap the cold, hard bread he'd eaten, he decided.

Distantly, he acknowledged her beauty. Flames of curly red hair framed a delicate porcelain face, tumbled down her back, and fell in ringlets over her breasts . . . breasts full and high and pink-tipped.

Legs of alabaster and rose; slender of ankle, generous of thigh. More shimmering red curls where they met. For a moment, he suffered an inexplicable inability to draw his gaze higher.

But only for a moment.

She clutched a tiny kitten to her breasts, and he had another strange moment, considering the wee beastie's lush perch, assailed by a vague and distant recollection.

It eluded him.

Unseelie females were icy creatures, with thin limbs and chill bodies.

Yet this woman didn't look icy. Nor slim. But full and generously rounded and soft and . . . warm.

It would be unwise to seek out the company of female humans or permit them to touch you, his king had ordered.

Vengeance turned his back and left the tower walk.

Jane's mouth opened and shut a dozen times while he stood at the top of the tower gazing down at her. He'd disappeared without a word. As if he didn't even know her! As if they hadn't been dream lovers for nearly forever!

As if she wasn't even standing there in all her glory, which—if one believed the love words he'd whispered in her dreams—was considerable.

Well, Jane Sillee thought irritably, *if he thinks this is a dream breakup, he's got another thought coming.*

Four

It was a little difficult to convincingly stomp into a castle nude, even in a dream.

One fretted about things like cellulite and what one's bare foot might stomp upon.

So Jane succeeded only, despite her righteous ire, in slinking into the castle, looking rather uncertain and, if her nipples were a weathervane, noticeably chilled.

He was sitting before the empty hearth, staring into it. She gazed at the fireplace wistfully, longing for a fire. It might be summer outside, but it was cold within the damp stone walls. Ever chivalrous in her dreams, he would surely accommodate her slightest wish and build a fire.

It occurred to her then that she'd never been cold in one of her dreams before. She filed the thought away for future consideration. There was something very odd about this dream.

"Aedan," she said softly.

He didn't move a muscle.

"Aedan, my love," she tried again. Perhaps he was in a bad mood, she thought, perplexed, although he'd never been in a bad mood in any of her dreams before, but she supposed there was a first time for everything. Was he angry at her for something? Had she popped in after committing some dream transgression?

He still didn't move or respond.

"Excuse me," she said not so sweetly, circling around in front of him, using the love-starved kitten as a shawl of sorts, feeling suddenly insecure, wondering what to cover, her breasts or her . . . Well, maybe he wouldn't look down.

He looked down.

When she lowered the mewing kitten, he looked up.

"That's not fair," she said, blushing. "Lend me your shirt." This was not unfolding like one of her dreams at all. Ordinarily, she didn't mind being nude with him because they were either making love in bed, or in a pile of freshly mown hay, or in a sweet, clear loch, or on a convenient table, but now he was fully clothed, and something was way off-kilter. "Please." She extended her hand.

When he shrugged, stood up, and began unlacing his linen shirt, her breath caught in her throat. When he raised one arm over his head, grabbed the nape of his shirt in a fist, and tugged it over his head, she swallowed hard. "Oh, *Aedan,*" she breathed. Gorgeous. He was simply flawless, with supple muscles rippling in his arms, his chest, and his taut abdomen. She'd kissed every smooth ripple in her dreams. The sheer, visceral beauty of her Highlander hit her like a fist in the stomach, making her knees weak.

"I know not why you persist in addressing me by that appellation. I am Vengeance," he said, his voice like a blade against rough stone.

Jane's mouth popped open in an "O" of surprise. "Vengeance?" she echoed blankly, round-eyed. Then, "This *is* a dream, isn't it, Aedan?" It was quite different from her usual dream. In her dreams everything was soft-focus and fuzzed around the edges, but now things were crystal clear.

A little too clear, she thought, frowning as she glanced around.

The interior of the castle was an absolute mess. Grime and soot stained the few furnishings, and cobwebs swayed from the rafters. There was no glass in the windows, no draperies, no sumptuous tapestries, no luxurious rugs. A lone rickety chair perched before a dilapidated table that tilted lopsidedly before an empty hearth. No candles, no oil globes. It was spartan, gloomy, and downright chilly.

He pondered her question a moment. "I doona know what dreams are." There was only existing as he had always known it. Shadows and ice and his king. And pain sometimes, pain beyond fathoming. He'd learned to avoid it at all cost. "But I am not who you think."

Jane inhaled sharply, hurt and bewildered. Why was he denying who he was? It was him . . . yet not him. She narrowed her eyes, studying him. Sleek dark fall of hair—same as in her dreams. Chiseled face and sculpted jaw—same. Brilliant eyes, the color of tropical surf—not the same. Frost seemed to glitter in their depths. His sensual lips were brushed with a hint of blueness, as if from exposure to extreme cold. Everything about him seemed chilled; indeed, he might have been carved from ice and painted flesh tones.

"Yes, you are," she said firmly. "You're Aedan MacKinnon."

An odd light flashed deep within his aquamarine eyes but was as quickly gone. "Cease with that ridiculous name. I am Vengeance," he said, his deep voice ringing hollow in the stone hall. He thrust his shirt at her.

Eagerly, she reached for it, intensely unsettled, needing clothing, some kind of armor to deflect his icy gaze. As her hand brushed his, he snatched his back, and the shirt dropped to the floor.

Doubly hurt, she stared at him a long moment, then stooped and placed the kitten on the floor, where it promptly twined about her ankles, purring. Fumbling in her haste, she swiftly slipped the shirt over her head and tugged it down as far as it would go. The soft fabric came nearly to her knees when she rose again. The neck opening dropped to her belly button. She laced it quickly, but it did little to cover her breasts.

His gaze seemed quite fixed there.

Taking a quick deep breath, she skirted the amorous kitten and stepped toward him.

Instantly, he raised a hand. "Stay. Doona approach me. You must leave."

"Aedan, don't you know me at all?" she asked plaintively.

"Verily, I've ne'er seen you before, human. This is my place. Begone."

Jane's eyes grew huge. "Human?" she echoed. "Begone?" she snapped. "And go where? I don't know *how* to leave. I don't know how I got here. Hell's bells, I'm not certain I really *am* here or even where here is!"

"If you won't leave, I will." He rose and left the hall, slipping into the shadows of the adjoining wing.

Jane stared blankly at the space where he'd been.

Jane studied the lake a long moment before dipping her finger in, then licking it. The tiger-striped kitten sat back on its haunches, twitching its wide fluffy tail and watching her curiously.

Salt. It was no lake she was surrounded by, but the sea. *What sea?* What sea abutted Scotland? She'd never been good with geography; she was lucky she could find her way home every day. But then again, she mused, never before in one of her dreams had she bothered to wonder about geography—more evidence that this dream was strikingly abnormal.

Jane dropped down cross-legged on the rocky shore, shaking her head. Either she'd gone completely nuts, or she was having her first-ever nightmare about her dream lover.

As she sat, rubbing her forehead and thinking hard, the soft syllables of a rhyme teased her memory. Something about saving him . . . about being in his century.

Jane Sillee, you've finally done it, she chided herself, *you've read one too many romance novels.* Only in books did heroines get swept back in time, and then they usually ended up in medieval—*oh!*

Lurching to her feet, she spun back toward the castle and took a long, hard look at her surroundings. To the left of the castle, some half mile in the distance, was a village of thatch-roofed, wattle, and daub huts, with tendrils of smoke curling lazily skyward.

A very medieval-looking village.

She pinched herself, hard. "Ow!" It hurt. She wondered if that proved anything. "It's not possible," she assured herself. "I *must* be dreaming."

Free him from his ice-borne hell and in his century you both may dwell. In the Dreaming hast thou loved him now, in the Waking must thou save him. The rhyme, elusive a few moments ago, now resurfaced clearly in her mind.

"Impossible," she scoffed.

But what if it isn't? a small voice in her heart queried hopefully. What if the mysterious tapestry had somehow sent her back to medieval times? Accompanied by pretty clear instructions: that if she could save him, she could stay with him. In *his* century.

What century was that?

Jane snorted and shook her head.

Still, that small voice persisted with persuasive logic, *there are only three possibilities: You're dreaming. You're crazy. Or you're truly here. If you're dreaming, nothing counts, so you may as well plunge right in. If you're crazy, well, nothing counts either, so you may as well plunge right in. If you're really here, and you're supposed to save him, everything counts, so you'd better hurry up and plunge right in.*

"I'm crazy," she muttered aloud. "Time travel, my ass."

But the small voice had a point. What did she have to lose by temporarily suspending disbelief and interacting with her surroundings? Only by immersing herself in her current situation might she be able to make any sense of it. And if it were a dream, eventually she'd wake up.

But heavens, she thought, inspecting the landscape, it all seemed so *real*. Far more real than any of her dreams had ever been. The dainty purple bell-shaped flowers exuded a sweet fragrance. The wind carried the tang of salt from the sea. When she stooped to pet the kitten, it felt soft and silky and had a wet little nose. If she was dreaming, it was the most detailed, incredible dream she'd ever had.

Which made her wonder how detailed and incredible making love with Aedan in this "dream" might be. That was incentive enough right there to plunge in.

Her stomach growled insistently, yet another thing that had never happened in one of her dreams. Resolutely, she turned back toward the castle. The kitten bounded along beside her, swiping at the occasional butterfly with gleeful little paws, then scurrying to catch up with her again.

She would keep an open mind, she resolved as she stepped inside the great hall. She would question him, find out what year it supposedly was, and where she supposedly was. Then she would try to discover why he didn't know her and why he thought he was "Vengeance."

Aedan sat again, as he had before, staring into the empty fireplace. Clad in loose black trousers, boots, and a gloriously naked upper torso, he was as still as death.

When she perched on the chilly stone hearth before him, his eyes glittered dangerously. "I thought you left," he growled.

"I told you, I don't know how to leave," she said simply.

Vengeance considered her words. Had his king deliberately placed the female human there? If so, why? Always before when his king had sent him into the mortal realm, Vengeance had been given precise instructions, a specific mission to accomplish. But not this time. He knew not what war to cause, whose ear to poison with lies, or whom to maim or kill. Mayhap, he brooded, this was his king's way of testing him, of seeing if Vengeance could determine what his king wanted of him.

He studied her. There was no denying it, he was curious about the human. She was the antithesis of all he'd encountered in his life; vibrant, with her flaming hair and curvy body. Pale porcelain skin and rosy lips. Eyes of molten amber fringed by dusky lashes and slanted upward at the outer corners. She had many facial expressions, lively muscles that pulled her lips up and down and many which ways. He found himself wondering what she would feel like, were he to touch her, if she was as soft and warm as she looked.

"Would you mind building me a fire?" she asked.

"I am not cold. Nor do you look cold," he added, his gaze raking over her. She looked far warmer than aught he'd seen.

"Well, I am. Fire. Now, please," she said firmly.

After a moment's hesitation, he complied with her command, layering the bricks, making swift work of it, never taking his gaze from her. He felt greatly intrigued by her breasts. He could not fathom what it was about those soft plump mounds beneath the worn linen that so commanded his attention. Were they on his own body, he would have been appalled by the excess fatty flesh, yet gazing upon her, he found his fingers clenching and unclenching, desirous to touch, perhaps cup their plump weight in his hands. For a

mere human, she had a powerful presence. He considered the
possibility that—wee as she was—she might be quite dangerous. After all, there were things in Faery minute of stature
capable of inflicting unspeakable pain.

"Thank you," she said, rubbing her hands together before
the blaze that sputtered in the hearth. "Those are peat bricks,
aren't they? I read about them once."

"Aye."

"Interesting," she murmured thoughtfully. "They don't
look like I thought they did." Then she shook her head
sharply and focused on him again. "What is the name of this
castle?"

"Dun Haakon," he replied, then started. Where had that
name come from? His king had told him naught about his
temporary quarters.

"Where am I?"

More knowledge he had no answers for: "On *Eilean A
Cheo.*"

"Where?" she asked blankly.

"'Tis Gaelic for 'misty isle.' We are on the Isle of Skye."
Mayhap it was knowledge his king had taught him long ago,
he decided. There, silent until needed. His king had oft told
him he'd prepared him for any place, any time.

Jane took a deep breath. "What year is it?"

"Fourteen hundred twenty-eight."

She inhaled sharply. "And how long have you lived here?"

"I doona live here. I am to remain but one passing of the
moon. I arrived yestreen."

"Where *do* you live?"

"You have many questions." He reflected for a moment,

34

and decided there was no harm in answering her questions. He was, after all, Vengeance. Powerful. Perfect. Deadly. "I live with my king in his kingdom."

"And where is that?"

"In Faery."

Jane swallowed. "Faery?" she said weakly.

"Aye. My king is the Unseelie king. I am his Vengeance. And I am perfect," he added, as if an afterthought.

"That's highly debatable," Jane muttered.

"Nay. 'Tis not. I am perfect. My king tells me so. He tells me I will be the most feared warrior ever to live, that the name of Vengeance will endure in legend for eternity."

"I'm quaking," Jane said dryly, with an aggrieved expression.

He looked at her then, hard. Her hair, her face, her breasts, then lower still, his gaze lingering on her smooth bare legs and slender ankles. "You are not at all what I expected of humans," he said finally.

Go with it, she told herself. *Since none of this makes any sense, just run with what he's told you and see where it leads.* "You aren't what I expected of a faery," she said lightly. "Aren't you supposed to have sparkly little wings?"

"I doona think I am a faery," he said carefully.

"Then you're human?" she pressed.

He looked perplexed, then gave a faint shake of his head.

"Well, if you're not a fairy and you're not human, what are you?"

His brows dipped and he shifted uncomfortably but made no reply.

"Well?" she encouraged.

After a long pause he said, "I will be needing my shirt back, lass. You may find clothing in the round tower down the corridor." He pointed behind her. "Go now."

"We're not done with this conversation, Aedan," she said, eyes narrowing.

"Vengeance."

"I'm not going to stop asking questions, *Aedan*. I have oodles of them."

He shrugged, rose, and wandered over to the window, turning his back to her.

"And I'm hungry, and when I get hungry I get grumpy. You do have food, don't you?"

He remained stoically silent. A few moments later he heard her snort, then stomp off in search of clothing.

If you're not a faery and you're not human, what are you? Her question hung in the air after she'd left, unanswered. Unanswerable.

Verily, he didn't know.

Five

S HE WAS A DEMANDING CREATURE.

Vengeance ended up having to make three trips into Kyleakin to acquire those things the lass deemed "the bare necessities." It was abundantly clear that she had no plans of leaving. Indeed, she intended to loll in the lap of luxury for the duration of her stay. Because he wasn't certain if his liege had arranged her presence as part of some mysterious plan he'd chosen not to impart, and because he'd been told to reside at the castle until summoned, it seemed he must share his temporary quarters. He was greatly uneasy and just wished he knew what was expected of him. How could he act on his king's behalf if he knew not why he was there?

On his first foray into Kyleakin—the only trip made of his own volition while she'd been occupied rummaging through trunks in the round tower—he'd purchased naught but day-old bread so they both might eat that eve. Although he found the heat and colors of the landscape chafing, he was relieved to escape her disconcerting presence and foolishly believed procuring food might silence her ever-wagging tongue.

When she discovered he'd "gone shopping" without informing her, she'd tossed her mass of shining curls and scowled, ordering him to procure additional items. The second time he'd spent a fair amount of the gold coin his liege had given him purchasing clean (so mayhap they were a bit scratchy and rough, but *he* didn't even need them to begin with) woolens, meat, cheese, fruit, quills, ink, and three fat, outrageously costly sheets of parchment—the parchment and quills because she'd proclaimed she was "a writer" and it was imperative she write every day without fail. At first he'd been puzzled by her bragging that she knew her letters, then he realized it was, like as not, a rare achievement for a mere mortal. He imagined he knew many more letters than she, and if she still needed to practice them, she was a sorry apprentice indeed.

Unimpressed with the results of his second expedition, she'd sent him back a *third* time, with a tidy little list on a scrap of parchment, to find more parchment, coffee beans or strong tea, a cauldron, mugs, eating tools, a supply of rags and vinegar for cleaning, *soft* woolens, down ticks, wine, and "unless you wish to fish the sea yourself," fresh fish for the useless furry beastie.

Vengeance, being ordered about by a wee woman. Fetching food for a mouse catcher.

Still, she was a mesmerizing thing. Especially in the pale pink gown she'd dug out of one of the many trunks. Her eyes sparkled with irritation or as she listed her demands, her breasts jiggled softly when she gestured, then she turned all cooing and tender as she stooped to scratch the beastie behind its furry ears.

Making him wonder what her slender fingers might feel like in his hair.

He was unprepared for one such as she and wondered why his king had not forewarned him that humans could be so . . . intriguing. None that he'd e'er encountered in his past travels had been so compelling, and his king had e'er painted them as coarse, sullen, and stupid creatures, easily manipulated by higher beings like Vengeance.

He'd not yet manipulated the smallest portion of his current circumstances, too busy being ordered about by her. *Build me a fire, give me your shirt, buy me this, buy me that. Hmph!* What might she demand next? He—the formidable hand of the faery king's wrath—was almost afraid to find out.

"Kiss me."

"What?" he said blankly.

"Kiss me," she repeated, with an encouraging little nod.

Vengeance stepped back, inwardly cursing himself for retreating, but something about the fiery lass made him itch to flee to the farthest reaches of the isle. At her direction, he'd fluffed several heavy down ticks on the sole bed in the keep. She was happily spreading it with soft woolens and a luxurious green velvet throw he'd not intended to buy. He'd been coerced into taking it by the proprietor, who'd been delighted to hear a woman was in residence at Dun Haakon and had eagerly inquired, "Be ye the new laird and lady of Dun Haakon?" Scowling, he'd flung coin at the shopkeeper, snatched up the bedclothes, and made haste from the establishment.

He was beginning to resent that his king had given him no orders. There, in his dark kingdom, Vengeance knew who he was and what his aim. Here, he was lost, abandoned in a stifling, garish world he did not understand, surrounded by creatures he could not fathom, with not one word of guidance from his liege.

And now the wench wanted him to do something else. Precisely what, he wasn't certain, but he suspected it boded ill for him. She was a creature greatly preoccupied with her physical comforts, and down that path—so his king oft said—lay weakness, folly, and ruin. Vengeance had few physical needs, merely food, water, and the occasional hour of rest.

"Kiss me," she said, making a plump pucker with her lips. She gave the velvet coverlet a final smoothing. "I think it might help you remember."

"What exactly is a kiss?" he asked suspiciously.

Her eyes widened and she regarded him with amazement. "You don't know what a kiss is?" she exclaimed.

"Why should I? 'Tis a mortal thing, is it not?"

She cocked her head and looked as if she were having a heated internal debate. After a moment she appeared to reach a decision and stepped closer to him. Stoically, he held his ground this time, refusing to cede an inch.

"I merely want to press my lips against yours," she said,

innocence knitted to a disarming smile. "Push them together, like so." She demonstrated, and the lush moue of her mouth tugged something deep in his groin.

"Nay. You may not touch me," he said stiffly.

She leaned closer. He caught a faint scent, something sweet and flowery on her fiery tresses. It made him want to press his face to her hair, inhale greedily, and stroke the coppery curls.

He leaned back. Fortunately, the lass was too short to reach his face without his cooperation. Or a step stool.

"You are so stubborn," she said, with a gusty sigh. "Fine, let's talk then. It's pretty clear we have a *lot* to talk about." She paused, then, "He doesn't know what kisses are," she muttered to herself, shaking her head. "*That's* never happened in my dreams before." Perching on the end of the bed, her feet dangling, she patted the space beside her. "Come. Sit by me."

"Nay." When the kitten jumped daintily onto the bed and spilled across the velvet coverlet, he scowled at it. "You or that bedraggled mop of fur—I'm fair uncertain which is more useless. At least the beastie doesna prattle on so."

"But the beastie can't kiss either," she said archly. "And it's not bedraggled. Don't insult my kitten," she added defensively.

"You attribute high value to these kisses of yours. I scarce believe they are worth much," he said scornfully.

"That's because you haven't kissed me yet. If you did, you'd know."

Vengeance moved, in spite of his best intentions, to stand at the foot of the bed between her legs. He stared down at her.

She scooped up the kitten and pressed her lips to its furry head. He closed his eyes and fought a tide of images that made no sense to him.

"Perhaps you're afraid," she said sweetly.

He opened his eyes. "I fear nothing."

"Then why won't you let me do something so harmless? See? The kitten survived unscathed."

He struggled with the answer for a moment, then said simply, "You may not touch me. 'Tis forbidden."

"Why not, and by whom?"

"I obey my king. And 'tis none of your concern why."

"I think it is. I thought you were a man who thought for himself. A warrior, a leader. Now you tell me you follow orders like some little puppet."

"Puppet?"

"An imitation of a real person fashioned of wood, pulled this way and that by its master. You're nothing but a servant, are you?"

Her delicate sneer cut him to the quick, and he flinched angrily. Who was she calling a servant? He was Vengeance, he was perfect and strong and ... *Och, he* was *his king's servant.* Why did that chafe? Why did he suffer the odd sensation that once he'd not been anyone's serf but a leader in his own right?

"Why do you obey him?" she pressed. "Does this king of yours mean so much to you? Is he so good to you? Tell me about him."

Vengeance opened his mouth, closed it again, and left the room silently.

"Where are you going?" she called after him.

"To prepare a meal, then you will sleep and leave me in peace," he growled over his shoulder.

Jane ate in bed, alone but for the kitten. Aedan brought her fish roasted over an open fire and a blackened potato that had obviously been stuffed in the coals to cook, accompanied by a similarly charred turnip, then left in silence. No salt. No butter for the dry potato. Not one drop of lemon for the fish.

Warily, she conceded that she was probably not dreaming—the fare had never been so unpalatable in one of her dreams. And upon reflection, she realized that although she'd attended many dream feasts, she'd never actually eaten anything at any of them. Now, she choked it down because she was too emotionally drained to attempt cooking for herself over an open fire. Tomorrow was another day.

The tiger-striped kitten, whom she'd christened Sexpot (after apologetically peeking beneath her tail) because of the way the little tyke sashayed about as if outrageously pleased with herself, hungrily devoured a tender fish filet, then busied herself scrubbing her whiskers with little spit-moistened paws while Jane puzzled over her situation.

She'd been astonished to discover Aedan had no idea what a kiss was, but the more she thought about it, the more sense it made.

Aedan not only didn't know he was Aedan, he didn't remember that he was a *man,* hence he didn't recall the intimacies of lovemaking!

She wondered if that made him a virgin of sorts. When they finally made love—and there was no doubt in her mind that they would, one way or another, even if she had to ambush and attack him—would he have any idea what it was all about? How strange to think that she might have to teach him, he who'd been her inexhaustible dream tutor.

He certainly hadn't liked being provoked, she mused. He'd grown increasingly agitated when she'd mocked him for obeying his king and had visibly bristled at the idea of being a mere servant. Still, despite such promising reactions, he had a formidable shell that was going to be difficult to penetrate. It would help if she knew what had happened to him. She needed to make him talk about his "king," and find out when and how they'd met. Were there indeed a "faery king," perhaps the being had enchanted him. The idea taxed Jane's credulity, but, all things considered, she supposed she couldn't suspend disbelief without suspending it fully. Until she reached some concrete conclusions about what was going on, she would be unwise to discount any possibilities.

Whatever had happened to him, she had to undo it. She hoped it wouldn't take too long, because she wasn't sure how long she could stand watching her soul mate glare at her with blatant distrust and dislike. Withholding kisses. Refusing to let her touch him.

You have one month here with him, no more, a woman's lilting voice whispered.

Sexpot stopped grooming, paw frozen before her face. She arched into a horseshoe shape and emitted a ferocious hiss.

"Wh-what?" Jane stammered, glancing about.

Cease with your absurd protestations that this place is not real.

44

You are in the fifteenth century, Jane Sillee. And here you may stay, if you succeed. You have but one full cycle of the moon in the sky to make him remember who he is.

Jane opened her mouth, closed it, and opened it again, but nothing came out. Sexpot suffered no such problem, growling low and long. Gently smoothing the spiked hairs on the kitten's back, Jane wet her lips and swallowed. "That's impossible, the man will hardly speak to me! And who are you?" she demanded. *I'm talking to a disembodied voice,* she thought, bewildered.

I'm not the one who doesn't know. Worry about him.

"Don't be cryptic. Who are you?" Jane hissed.

There was no reply. After a few moments, Sexpot's back no longer resembled a porcupine's, and Jane realized that whoever had spoken was gone.

"Well, just what am I supposed to do?" she shouted angrily. A month wasn't a whole lot of time to figure out what had happened to him and to help him remember who he was. She'd like to know who was making up the rules. She had a bone or two to pick with them.

Aedan appeared in the doorway, glancing hastily about the chamber. Only after ascertaining she was alone and in no apparent danger did he speak. "What are you yelling about?" he demanded.

Jane stared at him, framed in the doorway, gilded by a shaft of silvery moonlight that spilled in the open window, his sculpted chest bare, begging her touch.

She was suddenly stricken by two certainties that she felt in the marrow of her bones: that as the woman had said, she truly was in the fifteenth century, and that if she didn't help him remember, something terrible beyond her ability to imagine would become of him. Would he live and die the icy, inhuman creature he'd become? Perhaps turn into something even worse?

"Oh, Aedan," she said, the words hitching in her throat. All her love and longing and fear were in his name.

"I am *Vengeance*," he snarled. "When will you accept that?"

When he spun about and stalked from the chamber, Jane sat for a long time, looking around, examining everything anew, wondering how she could have thought for even a moment that she might be dreaming. The reason everything had seemed so real was because it *was* so real.

She fell back onto the bed and stared at the cobwebby ceiling through the shimmer of silent tears. "I won't lose you, Aedan," she whispered.

Hours later, Vengeance stood at the foot of the bed, watching her sleep. He'd passed a time of restless slumber on the floor in the hall and awakened intensely agitated. His rest had not been of the kind he'd known in Faery—an edgy, mostly aware state of short duration. Nay, he'd fallen into deep oblivion for far longer than usual, and his slumbering mind had gone on strange journeys. Upon awakening, his memory of those places had dissolved with the suddenness of a bubble bursting, leaving him with the nagging feeling that he'd forgotten something of import.

Troubled, he'd sought her. She was sprawled on her back, pink gown bunched about her thighs, masses of fiery curls about her face. The kitten of which she seemed strangely fond—and it was too stringy to be palatable over a fire, nor was it capable of useful labor, hence her interest in it baffled him—was also sprawled on its back and had managed to insinuate itself into her hair. Its tiny paws curled and uncurled while it emitted a most odd sound. A bit of drool escaped its thin pink lips.

Cautiously, Vengeance lowered himself onto the bed. The lass stirred and stretched but did not awaken. The kitten curled itself into a circle and purred louder.

Gingerly, Vengeance plucked up a ringlet of her hair and held it between his fingers. It shimmered in the moonlight, all the hues of flame: golden and coppery and bronze. It was unlike aught he'd seen before. There were more colors in a simple hank of her hair than had been in the entirety of his world until yesterday.

He smoothed the curl between his thumb and forefinger.

The kitten opened a golden eye and stared at Vengeance's dark hand.

It did not flee him, he mused, which confirmed he wasn't faery; for 'twas well known that cats loathed fairies. On the other hand, it didn't attempt to touch him, which he supposed meant he wasn't human either, for the thing certainly flung itself at the lass at every opportunity.

So what am I?

Sliding his hand beneath her tresses, he sneaked a quick glance at her. Her eyes were still closed, her lips slightly parted. Her breasts rising and falling gently.

Two hands.

It felt. So. Good.

There certainly was a lot of touching going on in this

place. Even the kitten seemed to crave it. And she—ah, *she* touched everything. Petted the beastie, stroked the velvety coverlet he'd procured in Kyleakin, and would have touched him a dozen times or more—he'd seen it in her eyes. *Kiss me,* she'd said, and he'd nearly crushed her in his arms, intrigued by this "pressing of the lips" she'd described. The mere thought of touching such warmth did alarming things to his body. Tentatively, he touched the tip of his index finger to her cheek, then snatched it away.

The kitten buried its pink nose in her hair. After a moment's pause, Vengeance did, too. Then rested his cheek lightly against it, absorbing the sensation against his skin.

Why do you obey him? Is he so good to you?

Vengeance tried to ponder that thought. His king was . . . well, his king. What right did Vengeance have to question whether his liege was good to him? It was not his place!

Why not? For the first time in centuries, unhampered by the constant coercion of the king's dark spells, an independent thought sprouted and thrust down a thick taproot in his mind. He had no idea whence such a blasphemous thought had come, but it had, and it defied his efforts to cast it out. Pain lanced through his head behind his eyes. Excruciating pressure built at his temples, and he clamped his hands to his ears as if to silence voices only he could hear.

Aedan, come quickly, I have something to show you. Da brought me a baby pine marten! A lass's voice, a lass who'd once been terribly important to him. A wee child of eight, about whom he'd fretted and tried to protect. *Mary, she'll be fine with the wee pet,* a man's voice said.

But we're sailin' out on the morrow, Mary protested. *'Tis wounded and might harm her without meanin' to.*

Aedan has a way with the wee creatures, and he'll watch o'er his sister.

"Aedan," he breathed, testing the sound of it on his tongue.

"Vengeance," he whispered after a moment.

Neither name fit him like skin on bones. Neither place he'd been—neither his land of ice nor this isle—felt like well-worn boots, broken in and suited to the heel.

He suffered a fierce urge to claw his way from his own body, so strange and ill-fashioned did it suddenly seem. In his king's land he knew who he was and what purpose he served. But here, och, here, he knew nothing.

Nothing but pain in places deep in his head and tingles in places deep in his groin.

Warily, he eyed the pale curves of her legs peeking from the hem of the gown. How smooth they looked . . . how warm.

He squeezed his eyes tightly shut, envisioning his beloved home with his king.

Be ye the new laird and lady of Dun Haakon? the shopkeeper queried brightly in his mind, obliterating his soothing image of ice and shadow.

"Nay," he whispered. "I am Vengeance."

Six

THE VILLAGERS DESCENDED UPON THE CASTLE AT DAY-break.

Jane awakened slowly, feeling disoriented and vulnerable. She'd not dreamed of Aedan, and if she'd suffered any remnants of doubts that she was in the fifteenth century before she'd fallen asleep, they were gone now. She'd never slept through an entire night without at least one dream of her Highland love.

At first she wasn't certain what had awakened her, then the clamor of voices rose in the hall beyond the open door of the bedchamber. High-pitched and excited, they were punctuated by stilted, grudging replies in Aedan's deep burr.

Swiftly she performed her morning ritual of positive reinforcement by announcing brightly to the empty bedchamber, "It's today! What better day could it be?" She'd read somewhere that such small litanies were useful in setting one's mood, so she recited it each morning without fail. Yesterday was a memory. Tomorrow was a hope. Today was another day to live and do one's best to love. In her estimation that was pretty much all a person could ask.

Kissing the drowsy kitten on the head, she slipped from the bed, quickly stripped off her wrinkled dress, then donned the simple yellow gown she'd unearthed yesterday while going through the trunks. She was looking forward to wearing it, because it was undeniably romantic with its low, laced bodice and flowing skirt. Coupled with the complete lack of undergarments in any of the trunks, she felt positively sinful. Ready for her man at any moment. How she hoped it would be today!

Casting a quick glance about the room, she narrowed her eyes thoughtfully. She was going to want a few more items from the nearby village, and soon, specifically a large bathtub and whatever medieval people used for toothpaste and soap. Lured by the hum of voices, she hurried from the bedchamber.

Vengeance backed against the hearth like a cornered animal. A dozen yammering villagers thrust baked goods and gifts at him and prattled nonstop about some legend and how delighted they were to have a MacKinnon back to watch over them. How they would serve him faithfully. How they planned to rebuild his castle.

Him—watch over them? He'd as soon sweep his hand and raze the room, leaving naught but bones and silence!

But he kept both his hands, and the fairy gifts of destructive power his king had given him, carefully behind his back, because he didn't know what the blethering hell his liege wanted. Rage simmered in his veins—rage at the villagers, rage at his liege—stunning him with its intensity. Then *she* sauntered in and some of the rage dissipated, ousted by discomfort of another sort, slightly more palatable but no less disconcerting.

She was a sunbeam flickering about the gloomy interior of the hall. As he watched in tense silence, she smiled and spoke and took the villagers' hands in hers, welcoming the entire ragamuffin lot of them into what had been, for a blissfully short time, *his* quarters alone. How and when had he so completely lost control of himself and his environ? he wondered. Was control something the Fates leeched away slowly over a period of time, or a thing instantaneously nihilated by the mere appearance of a female? Enter woman—exit order.

And och, how they were smiling at her, beaming and adoring, clearly accepting her as their lady!

"She's *not* a MacKinnon," he snapped. Best he swiftly disabuse them of the foolish notion that he was laird and she lady.

All heads swiveled to look at him.

"Milord," one of them said hesitantly after a pained pause, "'tis naught of our concern if ye've handfasted her or no. We're simply pleased to welcome ye both."

"Nor am *I* a MacKinnon," he said stiffly.

A dozen people gaped, then burst into uneasy laughter. An elderly man with silver hair, clad in russet trews and a linen shirt, shook his head and smiled gently. "Come," he beckoned, hastening from the hall into the adjoining wing.

Wholly irritated with himself for doing so, Vengeance

sought the lass's gaze. He was so accustomed to obeying orders that making simple decisions, like whether or not to follow the elder, paralyzed him. He despised the confusion he
felt, despised being left to his own devices. She stepped
toward him, looking as if she planned to tuck her hand
through his arm. Baring his teeth in a silent snarl, he spun
around and followed the old man. Better his own decisions,
he decided, than to rely upon *her*.

A few moments later, he stood in the round tower watching the elderly man remove dusty woolens draped over ob-
jects stacked behind an assortment of trunks near the wall.
The elder seemed to be looking for one item in particular,
and upon locating it, devoted much care to wiping it free of
dust. Then he swiveled it about and propped it in front of
him, where all could see.

Vengeance sucked in a harsh breath. The elder had un-
covered a portrait of a dark-haired girl sitting between a man
and a woman. The man bore an eerie resemblance to himself.
The woman was a beauty with wild blond tresses. But the
little girl—ah, merely gazing upon her filled him with pain.
He closed his eyes, his breathing suddenly rapid and shallow.

*But you canna leave me, Aedan! Ma and Da hae gone sailin'
and I canna bear to be alone! Nay, Aedan, dinna be leavin' me!
I've a terrible feelin' you willna be comin' back!*

But this "Aedan," whoever he was, had had to leave. He'd
had no choice.

Vengeance wondered who the man and child were and
how he knew of them. But such thoughts pained his head so
he thrust them from his mind. 'Twas none of his concern.

"'Tis Findanus and Saucy Mary, with their daughter,

Rose," the old man informed him. "They promised centuries ago that although the keep might be abandoned, one day a MacKinnon would return, the village would prosper, and the castle would be filled with clan again."

"I am *not* a MacKinnon," Vengeance growled.

The elder retrieved yet another portrait of three men riding into battle. Even Vengeance was forced to concede his resemblance to them was startling.

"'Tis Duncan, Robert, and Niles MacKinnon. The brothers were killed fighting for Robert the Bruce more than a century ago. The keep has stood vacant since. The remaining MacKinnon resettled easterly, on the mainland."

"I am no kin of theirs," Vengeance said stiffly.

The lass who'd invaded his castle snorted. "You look just like them. Anyone can see the resemblance. You're obviously a MacKinnon."

"'Tis an uncanny coincidence, naught more."

The villagers were silent for a time, watching their elder for a cue. The old man measured him for several moments, then spoke in a tone one might employ to gentle a wild animal. "We came to offer our services. We brought food, drink, and materials to rebuild. We will arrive each morn at daybreak and remain as yer servants 'til dusk. We pray ye choose to remain with us. 'Tis clear ye are a warrior and a leader. Whatever name ye go by, we would be pleased to call ye laird."

Vengeance felt a peculiar helplessness steal over him. The man was saying that whether he was MacKinnon or not, they needed a protector and they wanted *him*. He felt a simultaneous disdain, a sense that he was above it all, yet . . . a tentative tide of pleasure.

He longed to put a stop to it—to cast the villagers out, to force the female to leave—but not being privy to his king's purpose in sending him there, he couldn't, lest he undermine his liege's plan. It was possible that his king expected him to submit to a fortnight of mortal doings to prove how stoically he could endure and demonstrate how well he would perform amongst them in the future. There was also the possibility that since he was his king's emissary in the mortal realm, he might have future need of this castle, and his king *intended* the villagers to rebuild it. He shook his head, unable to fathom why he'd been abandoned without direction.

"Oh, how lovely of you to offer!" the lass exclaimed. "How kind you all are! We'd *love* your help. I'm Jane, by the way," she told the elder, clasping his hand and smiling. "Jane Sillee."

Vengeance left the tower without saying another word. *Jane.* He rolled the name over in his mind. She was called Jane. "Jane Sillee," he whispered. He liked the sound of it on his lips.

His head began to pound again.

"What's ailing him, milady?" Elias, the village elder, asked after Aedan had departed and introductions had been made all around.

"He suffered a fall and took a severe blow to his head," she lied smoothly. "It may be some time before he's himself again. His memory has suffered, and he's uncertain of many things."

"Is he a MacKinnon from one o' their holdings in the east?" Elias asked.

Jane nodded, ruing the lie but deeming it necessary.

"I was fair certain, there's no mistakin' the look," Elias said. "Since the battle at Bannockburn, they've left the isle untended, busy with their holdings on the mainland. Long have we prayed they would send one of their kin to stand for us, to reside on the isle again."

"And so they have, but he was injured on the way here and we must help him remember," Jane said, seizing the opportunity offered, grateful that she now had coconspirators. "Touch him frequently, although it may appear to unsettle him," she told them. "I believe it helps. And bring children around," she said, remembering how in her dreams Aedan had adored children. "The more the better. Perhaps they could play in the yard while we work."

"We? *Ye* needn't labor like a serf, milady," a young woman exclaimed.

"I intend to be part of rebuilding our home," Jane said firmly. *Our home*—how she liked the sound of that! She was gratified to see a glint of appreciation in the women's eyes. There were several approving nods.

"Also, I heard somewhere that familiar scents can help stir memories, so if you wouldn't mind teaching me to bake some things you think he might like, I'd be most appreciative. I'm afraid I'm not the best cook," she admitted. "But I'm eager to learn."

More approving nods.

Jane beamed. Her morning litany really did help: Today was turning out to be a fine day after all.

Seven

AND SO THEY SETTLED INTO A ROUTINE WITH WHICH Jane was pleased, despite Aedan's continued insistence that he was not a MacKinnon. Days sped by, too quickly for Jane's liking, but small progress was being made both with the estate and with the taciturn, brooding man who called himself Vengeance. Each day, Jane felt more at home at Dun Haakon, more at home with being in the fifteenth century.

As promised, each morning at daybreak, the villagers arrived in force. They were hard workers, and although the men departed in the late afternoon to tend their own small plots of land, the women and children remained, laboring cheerfully at Jane's side. They swept and scrubbed the floors; scraped away cobwebs; polished old earthenware mugs and platters, candlesticks, and oil globes; and aired out tapestries, hanging them with care. They repaired and oiled what furniture remained, stored beneath cloths saturated with the dust of decades.

Before long, the great hall sported a gleaming honey-blond table and a dozen chairs. The sole bed had been lav-ishly (and with much giggling by the women) covered with the plumpest pillows and softest fabrics the village had to offer. Sconces were reattached to the stone walls, displaying sparkling globes of oil with fat, waxy wicks. The women stitched pillows for the wooden chairs and strung packets of herbs from the beams.

The kitchen had fallen into complete rubble decades ago, and it would take some time to rebuild. After much thought, Jane decided it wasn't *too* risky to suggest the piping of water from a freshwater spring behind the castle and direct the con-struction of a large reservoir over a four-sided hearth, guar-anteeing hot water at a moment's notice. She also sketched plans for counters and cabinets and a massive centrally lo-cated butcher's block.

In the meantime, Jane was learning to cook over the open fire in the great hall. Each afternoon the women taught her a new dish. Unfortunately, each evening she ate it with a man who refused to eat anything but hard bread, no matter how she tried to tempt him.

Late into the twilight hours, Jane scribbled busily away before the fire, sometimes making notes, sometimes working on her manuscript, all the while peeking at Aedan over her papers and writing the future she hoped to have with him. She liked the laborious ritual of using quill and ink, the flames in the open hearth licking at her slippered toes, the hum of crickets and soft hooting of owls. She relished the complete absence of tires screeching, car alarms pealing, and planes flying overhead. In all her life, she'd never experienced such absolute, awe-inspiring stillness.

By the end of the first week of renovations, she'd begun to draw hope from Aedan's bewildered silence. Although he refused to speak to her, day by day he participated a bit more in the repairs to the estate. And day by day, he seemed a bit less forbidding. No longer did she see disdain and loathing in his gaze, but confusion and . . . uncertainty? As if he didn't understand his place and how he fit into the grand scheme of things.

Jane intended to use her mouth as wisely as possible. She learned in her psychology courses at Purdue that attacking "amnesia" head-on could drive the person deeper into denial, even induce catatonia. So after much hard thought, she'd decided to give Aedan two weeks of absolutely no pressure, other than acclimating to his new environment. Two weeks of working, of being silently companionable, of not touching him as she so longed to do, despite the misery of being with him but forbidden to demonstrate her love and affection.

After those two weeks, she promised herself the seduction would begin. No more baths in Kyleakin in one of the village women's homes. She would begin bathing before the fire in the hall. No more proper gowns in the evening. She would wear lower bodices and higher hems.

And so, Jane bided her time, cuddled with Sexpot in the luxurious bed, and dreamed about the night when Aedan would lay beside her and speak her name in those husky tones that promised lovemaking to make a girl's toes curl.

Aedan stood on the recently repaired front steps of the castle and stretched his arms above his head, easing the tightness in his back. The night sky was streaked with purple. Stars twinkled above the treetops, and a crescent moon silvered the lawn. Every muscle in his body was sore from toting heavy stones from a nearby quarry to the castle.

Although he'd learned to avoid pain in the land of shadows, the current aches in his body were a strangely pleasurable sensation. He'd refused to participate in the repairs at first, withholding himself in silent and aloof censure, but much to his surprise, as he'd watched the village men work, he'd begun to hanker to lift, carry, and patch. His hands had itched to get dirty, and his mind had been eager to redesign parts of the keep that had been inefficiently, and in places, hazardously constructed.

Pondering the three commands his king had given, he'd concluded there was nothing to prevent him from passing time more quickly by working.

When on the third day he'd silently joined the men, they'd worked with twice the vigor and smiled and jested more frequently. They asked his opinion on many things, leading him to discover with some surprise that he *had* opinions, and, further, that they seemed sound. They accepted him with minimal fuss, although they touched him with disconcerting frequency, clapping him on the shoulder and patting his arm.

Because they weren't females, he deemed it acceptable.

When they asked the occasional question, he evaded. He completely ignored the lass who doggedly remained in the castle, leaving only to traipse off to the village, from whence she returned clean and slightly damp.

And fragrant-smelling. And warm and soft and sweet-looking.

Sometimes, merely gazing upon her made him hurt inside.

Vengeance shook his head, as if to shake thoughts of her right out of it. With each passing day, things seemed different. The sky no longer seemed too brilliant to behold, the air no longer too stifling to breathe. He'd begun to anticipate working each day, because in the gloaming he could stand back and look at something—a wall recently shored up, steps relaid, a roof repaired, an interior hearth redesigned—and know it was his doing. He liked the feeling of laboring and rued that his king might deem it a flaw in his character, unsuitable for an exalted being.

And each day, when his thoughts turned toward his king, they were more often than not resentful thoughts. His king might not have bothered to inform him of his purpose at Dun Haakon, but the humans were more than willing to offer him ample purpose.

Purpose without pain.

Without *any* pain at all.

He had a blasphemous thought that took him by surprise and caused a headache of epic proportions that throbbed all through the night: He wondered if mayhap his king mightn't just forget about him.

Eight

SWIFTLY DID ONE BLASPHEMOUS THOUGHT BREED AN-
other, the next more blasphemous, making the prior seem
nearly innocuous. Swiftly did traitorous thought manifest itself in traitorous action.

It was on the evening of the eleventh day of his exile,
when she was laying her meal on the long table in the great
hall, that Vengeance began his fall from grace.

He'd labored arduously that day, and more than once his
grip had slipped on a heavy stone. Furthering his unease, wee
children from the village had played on the front lawn all
afternoon. The sound of their high voices, bubbling with
laughter as they chased a bladder-ball at the edge of the surf
or teased the furry beastie with woolen yarns, had reverber-
ated painfully inside his skull.

Now, he sat in the corner, far from the hearth, chewing
dispiritedly on hard bread. Of late, he'd been eating loaf after

loaf of it, his body starved by his daily labors. Yet no matter how much bread he consumed, he continued to lose mass and muscle and to feel lethargic and weak. He knew 'twas why his grip had slipped today.

Of late, when she spread the table with her rich and savory foods, his stomach roiled angrily, and on previous evenings, he'd left the castle and walked outdoors to avoid temptation.

But recently, indeed only this morning, he'd thought long and hard about his king's remark concerning sustenance and had scrutinized the precise words of his command.

You must eat, but I would suggest you seek only bland foods.

I would suggest.

It was the most nebulous phrase his liege had ever uttered. *I would suggest.* That was not at all how his king spoke to Vengeance. It made one think the king might be . . . uncertain of himself, unwilling, for some unfathomable reason, to commit to a command. And "bland." How vague was bland? An engraved invitation to interpretation, that word was.

After much meditation, Vengeance concluded for himself—a thing coming shockingly easier each day—that apparently his king had suffered some uncertainty as to how hard Vengeance might be laboring, so he'd been unable to anticipate what sustenance his body would require. Thus, he had "suggested," leaving the matter to Vengeance's discretion. As his king had placed such a trust in him, Vengeance resolved he must not return to his king weakened in body and risk inciting his displeasure.

When he rose and joined her at the table, her eyes rounded in disbelief.

"I will dine with you this eve," he informed her, gazing at her. Nay, lapping her up with his eyes. The tantalizing scent of roasted suckling pig teased his nostrils; the glorious rainbow hues of fiery-haired Jane clad in an emerald gown teased something he couldn't name.

"No bread?" she managed after an incredulous pause.

"'Tis not enough to sustain me through the day's labors."

"I see," she said carefully, as she hastened to lay another setting.

Vengeance eyed the food with great interest. She served him generous portions of roast pork swimming in juices and glazed with a jellied sauce, roasted potatoes in clotted cream with chive, some type of vegetable mix in yet another sauce, and thin strips of battered salmon. As a finishing touch, she added several ladles of a buttery-looking pudding.

When she placed it before him, he continued to eye it, knowing he'd not yet gone too far. He could still rise and return to his corner, to his bread.

I would suggest.

He glanced at her. She had a spoon in her mouth and was licking the clotted cream from it. That was all it took. He fell upon the food like a ravening beast, eating with his bare hands, shoving juicy, deliciously greasy pork into his mouth, stripping the tender meat from the bones with his teeth and tongue.

Christ, it was heavenly! Rich and succulent and warm.

Jane watched, astonished. It took him less than three minutes to devour every morsel she'd placed on his plate. His aquamarine eyes were wild, his sensual mouth glistening with juices from the roast, his hands—oh, God, he started licking his fingers, his firm pink lips sucking, and her temperature rose ten degrees.

Elation filled her. Although he'd never admitted that he'd been ordered to eat only bread, she'd figured it out herself. Each night while she'd dined, he'd shot furtive glances her way, watching her eat, eyeing the food with blatant longing, and a time or two, she'd heard his stomach rumble.

"More." He shoved his platter at her.

Happily, she complied. And a third time, until he sat back, sighing.

His eyes were different, she mused, watching him. There was something new in them, a welcome defiance. She decided to test it.

"I don't think you should eat anything but old bread in the future," she provoked.

"I will eat what I deem fit. And 'tis no longer bread."

Her lips ached from the effort of suppressing a delighted smile. "I don't think that's wise," she pushed.

"I will eat what I wish!" he snapped.

Oh, Aedan, Jane thought lovingly, fighting a mist of joyous tears, *well done.* One tiny crack in the façade, and she had no doubt that a man of Aedan's strength and independence would begin cracking at an alarming rate now that it had begun. "If you insist," she said mildly.

"I do," he growled. "And pass me that wine. And fetch another flagon. I feel a deep thirst coming on." Centuries of thirst. For far more than wine.

Aedan couldn't get over the pleasure of eating. Sun-warmed tomatoes, sweet young corn drenched with freshly churned butter, roasts basted with garlic, baked apples in delicate pastry smothered with cinnamon and honey. There were so many new, intriguing sensations! The fragrance of heather on the autumn breeze, the salty rhythmic lick of the ocean when he swam in it to bathe each eve, the brush of soft linen against his skin. Once, when no one had been in the castle, he'd removed his clothing and stretched naked on the velvet coverlet. Pressed his body into the soft ticks. Pondered lying there with *her,* but then he'd caught a rash from the coverlet that had made the part of him between his legs swell up. He'd swiftly dressed again and not repeated that indulgence. Unfortunately, the rash lingered, manifesting itself at odd intervals.

There were unpleasant sensations, too: sleeping on the hard, cold floor whilst she curled cozily in the overstuffed bed with the beastie. The tension of watching the lass's ankles and calves as she sauntered about. The sickness he felt in his stomach when he gazed upon the soft rise of her breasts in her gown.

He'd seen much more than that, yestreen, when the audacious wench had tugged a heavy tub before the fire and proceeded to fill it with pails of steaming water and sprinkle it with herbs.

He'd not comprehended what she was doing until she'd been as naked and rosy-bottomed as when she'd arrived at the castle a fortnight past, and then he'd been too stunned to move.

Feeling strangely nauseous, he'd finally gathered his wits and fled the hall, chased by the lass's soft derisive snort. He'd warred with himself on the newly laid terrace, only to return a quarter hour hence and watch her from the shadows of the doorway where she couldn't see him. Swallowing hard, endeavoring to slow his breathing, to stop the thundering of his blood in his veins, he'd watched her soap and rinse every inch of her body.

When his hands were trembling and his body aching in odd places, he'd closed his eyes, but the images had been burned into his brain. Thirteen more days, he told himself. Less than a fortnight remained until he could return to his king.

But with each day that passed, his curiosity about her grew. What did she ponder when she sat before the hearth staring into the flames? Why had she no man when the other village women did? Why did she watch him with that expression on her face? Why did she labor so over her letters? Why did she want him to touch her? What would come of it, were he to comply?

And the most pressing question of late, as his thoughts turned less often to his king and more often to that puzzling pain between his legs or the hollow ache behind his breastbone:

How long would he be able to resist finding out?

Nine

"WHAT ARE YOU WRITING?" AEDAN ASKED CASUALLY, HIS tone implying that he cared not what she replied, or even if she did.

Although her heart leaped, Jane pretended to ignore him. They sat in chairs at catty-corner angles near the hearth in the great hall; she curled near a table and three bright oil globes, he practically inside the hearth atop the blaze. He'd been surreptitiously watching her across the space of half a dozen feet for over an hour, and his question was the first direct one he'd asked of her since her arrival at Dun Haakon that didn't concern castle matters. Concealing a smile, she continued writing as if she hadn't heard him:

He rose from the chair so abruptly that it toppled over, crashing to the floor. His aquamarine eyes glittering with desire, he ripped the sheaf of papers from her hands and threw them aside. He towered over her, his intense gaze seeming to delve into her very soul. "Forget these papers. Forget my question. I want you, Jane," he said roughly. "I need you. Now." He began to strip, unlacing his linen shirt, tugging it over his head. He pressed a finger to her lips when she began to speak. "Hush, lass. Doona deny me. 'Tis no use. I will have you this night. You are mine, and only mine, for all of ever, then yet another day."

"Why another day?" she whispered against his finger, her heart hammering with nervousness and anticipation. She'd never been with a man before, only dreamed of it. And the dark Highlander standing before her was every inch a dream come to life.

He flashed her a seductive grin as he unknotted his plaid and let it slip down over his ~~taut buttocks~~ lean, muscular hips. Bracing his hands on the arms of her chair, he lowered his head toward hers. "Because not even forever with you will be enough to satisfy me, sweet Jane. I'm a greedy, demanding man."

"I said what are you writing?" His voice was tight.

His hard body glistened bronze in the shimmering light of dozens of oil globes. "I can't resist you, lass. God knows I've tried," he groaned, his voice low and taut with need. "I think about you day and night, I can't sleep for wanting you. 'Tis a madness I fear will never abate."

Jane swallowed a dreamy sigh and paused, quill poised above the paper. She arched a brow at him, outwardly calm while inwardly melting. His eyes flashing in his dark face, he coiled tensely in his chair, as if he might leap up at any moment. And pounce. *Oh, if only!*

"Why do you care?" she said with a shrug, trying to sound nonchalant. She was sick of being patient. She knew that the presence of the villagers, the laboring with his hands on what had once been his home, and his nocturnal spying upon her in the bath were beginning to take a toll. She'd been wise to take a passive role for the past two weeks, but it was time to be more proactive. She had twelve days, and she was *not* going to lose him.

"You do nothing without purpose," he said stiffly. "I merely wish to know your purpose in practicing your letters so faithfully each eve."

Jane pressed her quill to parchment again:

> *He tugged her up from the chair, crushing her body against the hard length of his own. Gazing into her eyes, he deliberately rocked his hips forward so she could feel his ~~huge cock~~ need. Hard and hot, ~~his impressive erection~~ he throbbed, pressing through the thin silk of her gown . . .*

Jane blew out a breath of pure sexual frustration—writing love scenes sure could be sheer torture for a girl with no man of her own—and placed the quill aside. Sexpot promptly jumped onto the small side table and attacked the feather, shaking it violently. Rescuing the quill before the kitten shredded yet another one, she hesitated before answering. She knew that one inadvertent misstep might drive him back into his rigid shell. He'd made it clear he would never permit her to touch him. She had to find a way to coax him to touch her.

"I'm not practicing my letters. I write stories."

"What kind of stories?"

Jane stared at him hungrily. He was so damned sexy sitting there. Only yesterday he'd taken to wearing a plaid for the first time since his arrival, saying it was cooler to work in. There he sat looking just like *her* Aedan, clad in crimson and black and no shirt. His upper body glistened with a faint sheen of sweat as he perched as close to the fire as he could get.

"You wouldn't understand any of it," she said coolly.

"Understand what?" he said angrily. "I understand many things."

"You wouldn't understand what I write about," she goaded. "I write about human things, things you couldn't possibly understand. Remember, you're not human," she pressed. "By the way," she added sweetly, "have you figured out yet what you actually *are*?" There, she thought smugly, he looked incensed. Her Aedan was a proud man and didn't like to be belittled. Over the past week he'd begun to display resentment toward anything resembling a direct order, which pleased her and made her suspect that he would defy her outright, were she to issue a firm command.

Anger and confusion warred behind his eyes. "I have been laboring with other humans. You doona know what I can and can't understand."

"*Never* read my stories," she said sternly. "They are private. It's none of your business, Aedan."

"So long as I am laird of this castle, everything is my—" He broke off with a stricken expression.

"Laird of this castle?" she echoed, searching his gaze. He hadn't even bothered to chastise her for calling him "Aedan."

He stared into her eyes a long moment, then said stiffly, "I meant that the villagers think I am, so if you're to live here, in what they think is my castle, you should abide by that perception, too. Or find another place to live, lass. That's all I meant," he snapped, then pushed himself angrily up from his chair. But at the doorway, he cast a glance over his shoulder so full of frustrated longing, so rife with desire, that it sent a shiver up her spine. It was plain to see that he was beginning to feel all the things he'd once felt, but couldn't understand them.

Much later, Jane scooped up her papers in one arm and Sexpot in the other. She knew *exactly* which scene of the manuscript she was working on to inadvertently leave lying about tomorrow.

Ten

The first time he kissed her slowly, brushing his lips lightly back and forth, creating a delicious sensual friction, until hers parted, yielding utterly. The second, deeper, even more intimately, and the third so possessively that it made her dizzy. His silky tongue tangled with hers. He fitted his mouth so completely over hers that she could scarcely breathe. If a kiss could speak, his was purring, "You are mine forever."

Subsequent kisses blended, wet and hot and intoxicating, one into another until her head was reeling. She trembled, burning with the scorching heat of desire.

She whimpered when he traced the curve of her jaw, down her neck to the top of her breast. His touch evoked a blend of lassitude and adrenaline that made her feel strong and weak at the same time. Soft and supple, yet close to aggression. Hot and needy and achy.

His aquamarine eyes promised lovemaking that would strip bare far more than her body. Gently slipping the sleeves of her gown from her shoulders, he bared her breasts to his hungry gaze. The chilly air coupled with the molten promise in his eyes made her breasts feel tight and achy. When he lowered his dark head and captured a ~~pouty~~ nipple in his mouth, she whimpered with pleasure. When he buried his face between her breasts, slipping her gown down over her hips, she pressed ~~her honeyed womanhood~~ against him, clinging.

His lips seared her sensitive skin. He scattered light kisses across her tummy, nipping and nibbling, then dropping to his knees before her.

She could barely stand, her knees so weak with desire, and when his hot tongue pressed to her hotter flesh, lapping sweetly at her ~~passion juices~~ most private heat, she nearly screamed with the exquisiteness of it.

Jane stood in the doorway of the great hall, a smile curving her lips, watching Aedan. Fifteen minutes ago, she'd informed him that she was going to take a quick nap before beginning preparations for their evening meal. She'd headed for the bedchamber, conveniently leaving a few pages of her manuscript lying beside the hearth, as if forgotten.

He'd nodded nonchalantly, but his gaze had betrayed him by drifting to the parchment. Shortly after retiring to the bedchamber, she'd crept back to the hall. He was standing by the fire, reading so intently that he didn't even notice her standing in the shadows of the stone doorway, watching as his eyes narrowed and his grip tightened on the parchment.

After a few minutes, he wet his lips and wiped beads of sweat from his forehead with the back of his hand.

"I feel quite rested now," she announced, striding briskly into the hall. "Hey!" she exclaimed, feigning outrage that he was snooping. "Those are my papers! I told you not to read them!"

His head shot up. His eyes were dark, his pupils dilated, his chest rising and falling as if he'd run a marathon.

He shook the parchments at her. "What are these . . . these . . . *scribblings*?" Vengeance demanded in a voice that should have been firm but came out sounding hoarse. His chest felt tight, that heavy part of him betwixt his legs . . . *och, Christ, it hurt!* Instinctively, he palmed it through the fabric of his kilt to soothe it, hoping the pain would diminish, but touching it only seemed to make it worse. Appalled, he removed his hand and glared at her. She seemed to find the gesture quite fascinating.

Jane cornered him and tried to grab the papers from his hand, but he held them above his head.

"Just give them back," she snapped.

"I doona think so," he growled. He stood looking at her, her jaw, her neck. Her breasts. "This man you write of," he said tensely, "he has dark hair and eyes of my hue."

"So?" she said, doing her best to sound defensive.

" 'Tis *me* you write about," he accused. When she made no move to deny it, he scowled. " 'Tis in no fashion a proper woman might write—" He broke off, wondering what he knew of proper women when he knew naught of female humans but what he'd learned from her. He studied her, trying to think, which was immensely difficult with parts of his body behaving so strangely. His breath was too short and shallow, his mouth parched, his heart pounding. He felt intensely alive, all his senses stirring . . . demanding. *Starving for touch.* "This pressing of the lips of yours makes one feel as if one is"—he glanced back at the papers—"burning with the scorching heat of desire?" He, who'd long been cold, ached to feel such heat.

"Yes—if a man's any good at it," she said archly. "But you're not a man, remember? It probably wouldn't work for you," she added sweetly.

"You doona know that," he snapped.

"Trust me," she provoked. "I doubt you have the right stuff."

"I doona know what this right stuff of yours is, but I know that I am formed like a man," he said indignantly. "I look as all the villagers do." He thought hard for a moment. "Verily, I believe I am more well formed than the lot of them," he added defensively. "My legs more powerful," he said, moving his plaid to display a thigh for her. "See? And my shoulders are wider. I am greater of height and girth, with no excess fatty parts." He preened for her, and it was everything she could do not to drool. More well formed? Sheesh! The man could drive the sales of *Playgirl* right through the roof!

"*What*ever," Jane said, purloining one of her teenage niece Jessica's most irritating responses, guaranteed to provoke, issued in tones that implied *nothing* he could say or do might interest her.

"You would do well not to dismiss me so lightly," he growled.

They stared at each other for a long tense moment, then

he glanced back at the parchment. "Regardless of whether I'm human or no, 'tis plain from your writings that you wish me to do such things to you." His tone challenged her to deny it.

Jane swallowed hard. Should she pretend to order him not to? Should she concede? She was on tricky terrain, uncertain what would push his buttons just a teeny bit further. He was so close to falling on her like a ravening beast—and God, how she wanted him to! As fate would have it, her very indecision provoked him correctly. As she hesitated, nibbling on her lower lip, a thing she did often while thinking hard, his gaze fixed there. His eyes narrowed.

"You *do* wish me to," he accused. "Else you would have denied it outright."

She nodded.

"Why?" he asked hoarsely.

"It will . . . er, make me happy?" she managed lamely, twirling a strand of hair around her finger.

He nodded, as if that were a fine excuse. After a moment's hesitation he croaked, "You wish this now? At this very moment? Here?" He fisted his hands, half crumpling the parchment. His blasted voice had risen and dropped again like a green lad's. He felt incomparably foolish. Yet . . . also as if he faced a moment of ineluctable destiny.

Jane's throat constricted with longing as she gazed at him. She wanted him every bit as much as she needed to breathe and eat. He was necessary to the care and feeding of her soul. She nodded, not trusting herself to speak.

Vengeance stood motionless, his mind racing. His king had ordered that he not permit a human female to touch him.

But he'd said nothing about *Vengeance* touching a human female. There was this thing inside him, this great gnawing curiosity. He wondered if there was such a thing as "burning with the scorching heat of desire," and if so, just how it might feel. "If I do this, you may not touch me," he warned.

"I can't touch you?" she echoed. "That's *so* ridiculous! Don't you wonder why your king made up that idiotic rule?"

"You will do as I demand. I will do this thing as you have written, only if you vow not to touch me."

"Fine," she snapped. *Anything* to get his hands on her. She'd cheerfully acquiesce to being tied to the bed, if she must. Hmmm . . . intriguing thought, that.

When he stepped forward, she tipped her head back and gazed up at him.

He glanced swiftly at the parchment, as if committing it to memory. "First, I am to brush my lips lightly across yours. You are to slightly part yours," he directed.

"I think we can play it by ear," she said, leaning minutely nearer, praying fervently that he wouldn't change his mind. She felt she might combust the moment he touched her, so long had she ached to feel his hands on her body.

He glanced back at the parchment with a look of alarm and confusion. "You mentioned naught of ears in your writing. Am I to do something with your ears, too?"

Jane nearly whimpered with frustration. Snatching the parchment from his hands, she said, "It's a figure of speech, Aedan. It means we'll figure it out as we go along. Just begin. You'll do fine, I promise."

"I'm merely trying to ascertain we both know our proper positions," he said stiffly.

The hell with proper, Jane thought, moistening her lips with her tongue and gazing up at him longingly. The last thing she wanted from him was *proper.* "Touch me," she encouraged.

Warily, he leaned closer.

Jane swayed forward, drawn like a magnet to steel. She wouldn't be satisfied until she was clinging to him like Saran Wrap. Although she was forbidden to out and out touch him, once he touched her, she certainly could press against him.

But still, he didn't move.

"Would you please just *start* already?"

"I am not quite certain I know what your 'most private heat' is," he admitted reluctantly. What was happening to him? he wondered. Complying with his demand, she was not touching him, but the tips of her breasts nearly brushed his chest, he could feel the heat of her body, and an alarming urgency flooding his.

"I'll help you find it," she assured him fervently.

"You're too short," he hedged.

It took Jane two seconds to retrieve the small footstool from beside the hearth, plop it down at his feet, and stand on it. It put them nose to nose, a mere inch apart.

She stared at him, heart thundering.

And he stared silently back.

Their breath mingled. His gaze dropped from her eyes to her lips. Back to her eyes, then lips again. He wet his lips, staring at her.

Jane kept her hands behind her back so she wouldn't touch him, knowing he'd use it as an excuse to leave. It was intensely intimate, such closeness without actually touching.

And the way he was looking at her—with such raw hunger and heat!

A small sound escaped her. He answered in kind, then looked startled by his involuntary groan. Jane scarcely dared breathe, waiting for him to move that last tiny half inch. His dark, raw sexuality coupled with his innocence of lovemaking was an irresistibly erotic combination. The man was an expert lover, of that she had no doubt, yet it was as if it were his first time ever, and each touch would be an undiscovered country to him.

She gave a quarter inch, and he met her halfway.

His lips touched hers.

God, they were cold! she thought, stunned. Icy.

God, she was warm, he thought, stunned. Blazing.

Fascinated, Vengeance pressed his mouth more snugly to hers. He knew he was supposed to use his tongue somehow, but wasn't certain he understood the mechanics of it.

"Taste me," she breathed against his lips. "Taste me like you would lick juice from your lips."

Ah, he thought, understanding. Mesmerized by the softness of her lips, he touched the tip of his tongue to them, running it over the seam, and when her lips parted, he tasted her like he was trying to remove a bit of cream from the center of a pastry.

She was infinitely sweeter.

And then his body seemed to take over, to understand something he didn't, and with a hoarse groan, he plunged his tongue into her mouth and crushed her against him, locking his arms securely behind her back. But that wasn't good enough, he quickly decided, he needed her head just so, so he slipped his hands deep into her hair and clamped her face firmly, kissing her until they were both breathless.

It was incredible, he marveled, stopping to stare at her. He touched a finger to his own lips; they were warm.

And she got prettier when he kissed her! he thought, awestruck. Her lips got all swollen and cushy-looking, her eyes sparkled like jewels, and her skin grew rosy. *He'd* done that to her, he thought, with pride. He could make a lass prettier merely by pressing his lips to hers. 'Twas a gift his king had ne'er told him he possessed. He wondered how much prettier she'd get if he touched his lips to her in other places.

"You are lovely, lass," he said in a voice utterly unlike his own normal tone—indeed, it came out raspy and thick. "Nay, doona speak, I haven't finished."

He pressed his lips to hers again, swallowing her words. With butterfly light touches, his thumbs caressed smooth circles on the delicate skin of her neck, along the line of her jaw, and over her face. Then he drew back and ran his fingers lightly over her face, as if he were blind, absorbing the feel of every plane and angle from the downy soft brows to the pert nose and high bones of her cheeks, from the shape of her widow's peak to the point of her chin.

Her soft, lush lips.

When he rested a finger there too long, she gently sucked the tip of it, and heat lanced straight down to his groin. The vision of her lips closed full and sweetly around his finger near made him crazed . . . reminded him of something else, long forgotten, something a lass might do that was sweeter than heaven. His breath caught in his throat.

She stared at him, her amber eyes glowing, wide, trusting,

her lips around his finger. It made him nearly mad with some kind of pain in his breast.

Taking her face between his hands, he kissed her as if he could suck the heat of her right into his body, and indeed, it seemed he did. "I want to touch you 'til your skin smells of me," he growled, not knowing why. "Every inch of it."

But Jane understood. It was a purely male way of marking his territory, loving his woman until she bore his unique scent from head to toe. She whimpered assent into his mouth, her hands curled into fists behind her back because it was killing her to not touch him.

Then he lifted her from the stool, crushing her against him completely, holding her weight as if she were light as a feather, and his hard, hot arousal pressed into the vee of her thighs.

I'm dying, Vengeance realized dimly. The feel of her body against that swollen part of him that seemed to have never recovered from whatever rash he'd caught from the coverlet burned and throbbed angrily. He must be dying, because no man could withstand such pain for long.

Mayhap, he thought, once he'd undressed her as she'd directed in her parchments, he could doff his tartan, too, and she might tell him what was wrong with him.

But nay—he would press his lips to hers a few more times, for she might see the thing betwixt his legs and be disgusted. Flee him. For now, he was warm . . . so warm. He slipped his hands from her hair and down over her breasts. He shuddered, once, twice, and three times, before losing complete control of himself.

He had no idea what he'd done, lost to a madness of sorts,

until he stood looking at her as she perched atop the small stool naked, tatters of her dress scattered across the floor. He had no clear memory of ripping her gown away, so urgent and fierce had his need been to bare her completely to his touch.

"Did I hurt you?" he demanded.

Jane shook her head, her eyes wide. "Touch me," she encouraged softly. "Find my most private heat. You may look for it wherever you wish," she encouraged, eyes sparkling.

He circled her slowly. She didn't move a muscle, merely stood naked on the stool as he marveled over every inch of her. And when he returned to face her, he sucked in a breath. She'd done it again—grown more beautiful. Her eyes were filled with some lazy, dreamy knowing he could only guess at. Glittering and sleepy and desirous, her skin flushed from head to toe.

He reached out with both hands and gathered the firm, plump weight of her breasts in his palms. They felt sweet, so sweet. Their eyes met and she made a soft mewing sound that shivered through him.

"Kiss—"

"Aye," he said instantly, knowing what she wanted, and lowered his head to the soft pillows of her breasts. Unable to comprehend why he wanted it so badly, he closed his lips over first one nipple, then the next. Not knowing why he did it, his hand slipped between her soft thighs, sought the warmth and wetness . . .

And images assaulted him—he was someone else—a man who knew much of soft thighs and heated loving. A man who'd lost everything, everyone:

"Aedan, please dinna go!" the child sobbed. "At least wait 'til Ma and Da come home!"

"I must go now, little one." The man crushed her in his arms, *brushing helplessly at her tears. "'Tis only for five years. Why you'll be but a lass of ten and three when I return." The man closed his eyes. "I left a note for Ma and Da . . ."*

"Nay! Aedan. Dinna leave me," the child said, weeping as if her heart would break. "I love you!"

"Ahhh!" Vengeance roared, thrusting her away, clutching his head with both hands. He bellowed wordlessly, backing away until his spine hit the wall.

"Aedan! What is it?" Jane cried, jumping off the stool and scurrying toward him.

"Doona call me that!" he shouted, his palms clamped to his temples.

"But Aedan—"

"*Haud yer wheesht,* woman!"

"But I think you're remembering," she said frantically, trying to touch him, to soothe him.

Another wordless bellow was his only reply as he raced from the hall as if all the hounds of hell were nipping at his heels.

Eleven

ABOVE ALL ELSE, IT WOULD BE UNWISE TO SEEK THE company of female humans or permit them to touch you.

It would be unwise.

How had he overlooked such nonspecific phrasing?

It would be unwise. Vengeance didn't feel particularly wise at the moment. Nor did he intend to eat bland food, nor did he intend to circumvent Kyleakin because "it might be best."

Just as he'd begun to suspect, his king had, in truth, not issued a single order at all.

How and when did I meet him? Vengeance wondered for the first time. Had he been born in Faery, pledged to the king from birth? Had he met him in later years? Why couldn't he *remember*?

Vengeance sat in silence beside the gently lapping ocean, slapping the blade of a dirk against his palm.

Fae didn't bleed. They healed too quickly.

Vengeance made a fist around the blade.

Blood seeped from his clenched hand and dripped down the sides. He spread his fingers and studied the deep cuts.

They remained deep, oozing dark crimson blood.

A harsh, relieved breath escaped him.

How old was he? How long had he lived? Why could he not recall ever changing? Why did humans gray on their heads, yet Vengeance remained unchanged?

Nothing changes in Faery.

If he never went back, would his long black hair one day turn silver, too? Strangely, the thought appealed to him. Thoughts of a child rose unbidden in his mind. He imagined hugging one of the wee village lasses in his arms, wiping away her tears. Teaching her to climb trees, to make boats out of wood and sail them in the surf, bringing her a litter of mewing kittens whose mother had died birthing them.

"Who am I?" Vengeance cried, clutching his head.

It occurred to him that, in truth, mayhap the right question was—who had he once been?

Jane watched him from the front steps of the castle. He sat with his back to her in the deepening twilight, clutching his head, staring out to sea. Blood was smeared on one of his hands, dripping down his arm. Suddenly he stood up, and she caught a gleam of silver as he flung a blade, end over end, into the waves.

A salty breeze whipped at his hair, tangling the dark strands into a silken skein. His plaid flapped in the breeze, hugging the powerful lines of his body.

He seemed dark and desolate and strong and utterly untouchable.

Jane's eyes misted. "I love you, Aedan MacKinnon," she told the wind.

As if the wind eagerly whisked her words down the front lawn to the sea's edge, Aedan suddenly turned and looked straight at her. His cheeks gleamed wetly in the fading light.

He nodded once, then turned his back to her and walked off down the shore, head bowed.

Jane started after him, then stopped. There'd been such desolation in his gaze, such loneliness, yet a great deal of anger. He'd turned away, clearly demonstrating his wish to be alone. She didn't want to push him too hard. She couldn't even begin to understand what he was going through. She was elated that he was remembering and equally anguished by the pain it was causing him. She watched, torn by indecision, until he disappeared around a bend in the rocky shoreline.

Twelve

He didn't come back for three days. They were the most agonizing three days of Jane Sillee's life.

Daily, she cursed herself for pushing him too far too fast. Daily, she berated herself for not going after him when he'd begun walking down that rocky shore.

Daily, she lied to the villagers when they came to work, assuring them he'd only gone to see a man about a horse and would return anon.

And nightly, as she curled with Sexpot in the bed that was much too large for just one lonely girl, she prayed her words would prove true.

Thirteen

I T WAS THE MIDDLE OF THE NIGHT WHEN AEDAN RE-turned.

He awakened her abruptly, stripping the coverlets from her naked body, sending Sexpot flying from the bed with a disgruntled meow.

"Aedan!" Jane gasped, staring up at him. His expression was so fierce that her sleep-fogged brain cleared instantly.

He stood at the foot of the bed, his dark gaze sweeping every inch of her nude body. He'd braided his hair. His face was dark with the stubble of a black beard, shadowing his jaw. In the past few weeks, he'd lost weight, and although he was still powerfully muscular, there was a leanness to him, a dangerously hungry look, like a wolf too long alone and unfed in the wild.

He didn't say a word, just stripped off his shirt and kicked off his boots, then moved toward her.

89

She never would have believed it of herself, but he radiated such barely harnessed fury that she scuttled back against the headboard and crossed her arms over her breasts protectively.

"Och, nay, lass," he said with silky menace. "Not after all the times you've tried to get me to touch you. You willna nay-say me now."

Jane's eyes grew huge. "I-I—"

"Touch me." He unknotted his plaid and let it fall to the floor.

Jane's jaw dropped. "I-I—" she tried again, and failed, again.

"Is something wrong with me?" he demanded.

"N-No," she managed. "Uh-uh. No way." She swallowed hard.

"And this?" He palmed his formidable erection. "This is as it should be?"

"Oh," Jane breathed reverently. "Absolutely."

He eyed her suspiciously. "You're not just saying that, are you?"

Jane shook her head, her eyes wide.

"Then give me those kisses of yours, lass, and be quick about it." He paused a moment, then added in a low, tense voice, "I'm cold, lass. I'm so cold."

Jane's breath hitched in her throat and her eyes misted. His vulnerability melted her fears. She rose to her knees on the bed and extended her hands to him.

Never breaking eye contact, staring into her eyes as if the invitation in them was all that was sustaining him, he placed his hands slowly in hers and let her pull him onto the bed, where he knelt facing her.

She glanced down at their entwined hands, and his gaze followed. Her hands were small and white, nearly swallowed by his work-roughened and tan fingers. She flexed her fingers against his, savoring the first *real* feel of holding Aedan's hand. Until that moment, she'd only touched him in her dreams. She closed her eyes, savoring every bit of it, drinking the experience dry.

She opened them to find him regarding her with expectancy and fascination.

"Sometimes I think I know you, lass."

"You do," she said, with a little catch in her voice. "I'm Jane." *Your* Jane, she longed to cry.

He hesitated a long moment. Then, "I'm Aedan. Aedan MacKinnon."

Jane stared at him wonderingly. "You've remembered?" she exclaimed. "Oh, Aedan—"

He cut her words off with a gentle finger against her lips. "Does it matter? The villagers think I am. You think I am. Why should I not be?"

Jane's heart sank again. He still didn't recall.

But . . . he was here, and he was willing to let her touch him. She would take what she could get.

"Jane," he said urgently, "am I truly as a man should be?"

"*Everything* a man should be," she assured him.

"Then teach me what a man does with a woman such as you."

Aw, her heart purred. The look in his eyes was so innocent and hopeful, nearly masking the ever-present despair in his gaze.

"First," she said softly, raising his hand to her lips, "he

kisses her, like so." She planted a sweet kiss in his palm and closed his fingers over it. He did the same with both her hands, lingering over the sensitive skin of her palm.

"Then," she breathed, "he lets her touch him *all* over. Like this." She slid her hands up his muscular arms and into his hair. Removing his leather thong, she combed her fingers through the plait until it fell dark and silky around his face. She laid her palms against his face, staring into his eyes. He was still beneath her touch, his eyes unfocused.

"More," he urged, a stray tomcat, starved for touch.

"And she touches him here," she said, skimming his shoulders, the muscles of his back, down over his lean hips, and back up his magnificent abs and muscled chest. Unable to resist, she dropped her head forward against his chest and licked him, tasting the salt of his skin.

A rough groan escaped him, and the heat of his arousal throbbed insistently against her thigh.

Jane whimpered at the contact and pressed against him. She tasted his neck, his jaw, his lips and buried her hands in his hair. "Then, he brushes his lips—"

"I know this part," he said, sounding pleased with himself.

Fitting his mouth to hers, he kissed her; a deep, starving-soul kiss, and dragged her hard against his body.

The feel of her naked body against his bare skin made his head swim. Made him burn. Made him tremble with wonder. He'd never known . . . he'd never suspected what pleasure was to be found in touch. The feel of her wee hands on his body made him hotter than any fire could and brought him crashing to his knees inside himself.

She'd said that he was fashioned as a man should be, and she touched him as if she desperately craved his body. He liked that. It made him feel . . . och, just feel and feel and *feel*.

He nibbled and suckled at her lips, then plunged his tongue deeply, thrusting. His body moved to a rhythm, innate and primal. She went supple in his arms, dropping back onto the bed, and he followed, stretching his body atop her lush softness. "Christ, lass, I've ne'er felt aught such as you!" Intoxicated, he kissed her deeply, his silky hot tongue tangling with hers. When she shifted her legs beneath him, the swollen part of him was suddenly flush between her thighs, and he thrust against her instinctively. She raised her hips, pressing back, and he thought he would die from such sensation. He cupped her bottom and pulled her more firmly against him. Digging his fingers into the softness of her bare bottom filled him with a wild and fierce sensation—an urge to possess, to hold her beneath him until she wept with pleasure. Until he shuddered atop her. Images came to him then:

Of a man and a woman rolling naked across a bed. Of the firm pistoning motion of a man's hips, of slender ankles and calves raised near a woman's breasts, of the musky scent of skin and bodies, the sweat and rawness and heat of—

"*You have no clan. You have no home,*" the dark king said.

"*Nay, I do! I have clan all o'er the Highlands. My Highlands. My home.*" '*Twas the thought of his clan that sustained him. Along with yet a more exquisite thought—but the king had tried to steal that other, most important thought from him, so he'd built a tower of ice around it to keep it safe.*

"*Everyone in your clan died a hundred years ago, you fool. Forget!*"

"Nay! My people are not dead." But he knew they were.
Naught but dust returned to the Highland soil.

*"Everyone for whom you cared is dead. The world goes on
without you. You are my Vengeance, the beast who serves my bid-
ding."*

*And then the darker images, as the pain, the unending pain
began . . . and went on and on until there was nothing left but a
single frozen tear and ice where once had beat a heart that held
the hallowed blood of Scottish kings.*

He pushed her away, roaring.

Stunned, Jane fell back on the bed. Bewildered by his
abrupt leave-taking, she stammered, "Wh-What—" She
shook her head, trying to clear it, to understand what was
happening. One minute he'd been about to make wildly passionate love to her, the next he was five feet away, looking
horrified. "Why did you stop?"

"I can't do this!" he shouted. "It hurts too much!"

"Aedan—it's just—"

"Nay! I canna, lass!" Eyes wild, trembling visibly, he
turned and stormed from the bedchamber.

But not before she saw the remembering in his dark gaze.

Not before she saw the first faint hint of awareness of who
and what he really was.

"Oh, you know," she breathed to the empty room. "You
know." Chills shivered down her spine.

And he did. She'd seen it in his gaze. In the pain etched in
his face, in the stiffness of his body. He'd left her, moving like
a man who'd gone ten rounds in the ring, whose ribs were
bruised, whose body was contused from head to toe.

She had the sudden terrifying feeling that he might leave

94

her, that he might simply go back to his king so that he wouldn't have to face what he would now have to face.

"Aedan!" she cried, leaping up from the bed and chasing after him.

But the castle was empty. Aedan was gone.

Fourteen

JANE TROD DISPIRITEDLY INTO THE CASTLE, SHOUL-
ders slumped. It had been a week since Aedan had left, and
she had only two more days before . . . before . . . whatever
was going to happen would happen. She had no idea exactly
what would come to pass, but she was pretty certain he would
be gone from her, forever.

No longer in this castle. No longer even in her dreams.

Leaving her to a life of what? Only memories of dreams
that *nothing* could ever compare to.

Reluctant to go in search of him, in case he returned only
to find *her* gone, she'd been crying off and on for a week.
She'd barely been able to converse with the villagers when
they came to labor every day. The castle was progressing, but
to what avail? Both the "laird and lady" would likely be gone
in a matter of forty-eight hours, no more. How she would
miss this place! The wild rugged land, the honest, hard-

working people who knew how to find joy in the smallest of things.

Sniffing back tears, she mewed for Sexpot who, for a change, didn't come scampering across the stone floor, tail swishing flirtatiously.

Glancing around with tear-blurred eyes, she drew up short.

Aedan was sitting before the hearth, feet resting on a stool, with Sexpot curled on his lap.

As if him being there, petting the "wee useless beastie" wasn't astonishing enough, he'd propped the painting Elias had unearthed weeks ago against the table facing him and was staring at it.

She must have made some small sound, because without looking up, hand moving gently over the kitten's silvery fur, he said, "I walked about the Highlands a bit. One of the villagers was kind enough to ferry me to the mainland."

Jane opened her mouth, then closed it again. Such intense relief flooded her that she nearly crumpled to her knees. She still had two more days to try. *Thank you, God,* she whispered silently.

"Much has changed," he said slowly. "Little was familiar to me. I lost my bearings a time or two."

"Oh, Aedan," she said gently.

"I needed to know this place again. And . . . I suppose . . . I needed time."

"You don't have to explain," she hastened to assure him. The mere fact that he'd returned was enough. She'd nearly given up hope.

"But I do," he said, staring fixedly at the portrait. "There

is much I need to explain to you. You have a right to know.
That is," he added carefully, "if you still wish to share these
quarters with me."

"I still wish to share these quarters, Aedan," she said instantly. Some of the tension seemed to leave his body. How
could she make him understand that she wished not only to
share "quarters" but her body and her heart? She longed to
share *everything* with him. But there was something she had
to know, words she needed to hear him say. "Do you know
who you are yet?" She held her breath, waiting.

He looked at her levelly, a bittersweet smile playing
faintly upon his lips. "Och, aye, lass. I am Aedan MacKinnon.
Son of Findanus and Mary MacKinnon, from Dun Haakon
on the Isle of Skye. Born in eight hundred ninety-eight.
Twice-removed grandson of Kenneth McAlpin. And I am
the last of my people." He turned his gaze back to the portrait.

His words, delivered so regally, yet with such sorrow, sent
a chill up her spine. "Beyond that, you need only tell me what
you wish," she said softly.

"Then I bid you listen well, for I doona ken when I may
have the will to speak it again." That said, he grew pensively
silent and gazed into the fire, as if searching for the right
words.

Finally, he stirred and said, "When I was a score and ten
a . . . man of sorts . . . came to this castle. At first, I thought
that he'd come to challenge me, for I was heralded the most
powerful warrior in all the isles, descended from the mighty
McAlpin himself. Mayhap I was a bit pleased with myself."
He grimaced self-deprecatingly.

"But this man . . ." He trailed off shaking his head. "This man—he terrified even me. He looked like a man, but he was dead inside. Ice. Cold. Not human, but human. I know that doesn't make sense, but 'twas as if all the life had been sucked from him somehow, yet still he breathed. I feared he would harm my people and mock me while doing so. He was great and tall and wide, and he had powers beyond mortal."

When he paused, lost in his memories, Jane whispered, "Please go on."

He took a deep breath. "Ma and Da were away at sea with all my siblings but the youngest. I was here with my wee sister." He gestured to the portrait. "Rose." He closed his eyes and rubbed them. "Although I may have suffered my share of arrogance, lass, all I'd e'er wished for was a family, children of my own, to watch my sisters and brothers grow and raise their children. To live a simple life. To be a man of honor. A man that when he was laid into the earth, others said, 'He was a good man.' Yet on that day, I knew that such things would ne'er come to pass, for the man who'd come for me threatened to destroy my entire world. *And I knew he could do it.*"

Eyes misting, Jane hurried to him, sank onto the footstool, and placed a gentle, encouraging hand on his thigh.

He covered it with his own, staring at the portrait.

After a few moments, he turned his head and looked at her, and she gasped softly at the anguish in his eyes. She wanted to press kisses to his eyelids as if to somehow kiss all the pain away, to make sure nothing ever hurt him again.

"I made a deal with the creature that if he left my clan in

peace I would go with him to his king. His king offered a bargain and I accepted, thinking five years would be a hellish price to pay, wondering how I could withstand five years in his icy, dark kingdom. But it was ne'er five years, lass—'twas five hundred. Five hundred years and I forgot. I *forgot*." He slammed a fist down on the arm of the chair. Thrusting the kitten at her, he leaped to his feet and began pacing. Sexpot, alarmed by the sudden commotion, scampered off for the calm of the bedchamber.

"I became just like him—the one who'd come to claim me. I lost all honor. I became the vilest of vile, the—"

"Aedan, stop," Jane cried.

"I became that thing I despised, lass!"

"You were tortured," she defended. "Who could survive five centuries of . . . of . . ." She trailed off, not knowing what he'd withstood.

Aedan snorted angrily. "I let them go. To escape the things that the king did to me. I let memories of my clan, of my Rose, go. The more I forgot, the less he punished me. God, there are things in the dark king's realm, things so . . ." He snarled, shaking his head.

"You *had* to forget," Jane said intensely. "It's a miracle that you survived. And although you might think you became this Vengeance creature who came for you—you *didn't*. I saw the goodness in you when I came here. I saw the tenderness, the part of you that was aching to be a simple man again."

"But you doona know the things I've done," he said, his voice harsh and deep and unforgiving.

"I don't need to know. Unless you wish to tell me, I need

never know. All I need to know is that you are never going back to him. You're never going back to him, are you?" Jane pressed.

He said nothing, just stood there, looking lost and full of self-loathing. His head bowed, his hair curtaining his face.

"Stay with me. I want you, Aedan," she said, her heart aching.

"How *could* you? How could anyone?" he asked bitterly.

Ah, she thought, understanding. He hungered to be part of the mortal world—that was why he'd come back to Dun Haakon, rather than turning to his king—but he felt he didn't deserve it. He feared no one would want him, that once she knew what he'd been, she would cast him out.

He glanced at her, then quickly glanced away, but not before she saw the hope warring with the despair in his gaze.

Rising to her feet, Jane held out her hand. "Take my hand, Aedan. That's all you need do."

"You doona know what these hands have done."

"Take my hand, Aedan."

"Begone, lass. A woman such as you is not for the likes of me."

"Take my hand," she repeated. "You can take it now. Or ten years from now. Or twenty. Because I will still be standing here waiting for you to take my hand. I'm not leaving you. I'm *never* leaving you."

His anguished gaze shot to hers. "Why?"

"Because I love you," Jane said, her eyes filling with tears. "I love you, Aedan MacKinnon. I've loved you forever."

"Who are you? Why do you even *care* about me?" His voice rose and cracked hoarsely.

"You still don't remember me?" Jane asked plaintively.

Aedan thought hard, pushing into the deepest part of him, that part that still was iced over. A hard shining tower of ice still lay behind his breast, concealing something. Helplessly, he shook his head.

Jane swallowed hard. It didn't really matter, she told herself. He didn't have to remember their time together in the Dreaming. She could live with that, if it meant she could spend the rest of her life here on this island with him. "It's okay," she said finally with a brave smile. "You don't have to remember me, as long as you—" She broke off abruptly, feeling suddenly too vulnerable for words.

"As long as I what, lass?"

In a small voice, she finally said, "Do you think you could care for me? In the way a man cares for his woman?"

Aedan sucked in a harsh breath. If only she knew. For the week he'd wandered, he'd thought of little else. Knowing he should do her the favor of never returning, yet unable to stay away. Dreaming of her, waking to find his arms reaching for nothing. Until, unable to push her from his heart, he'd faced his memories. Until, scorning himself for a fool, he'd returned to Dun Haakon to force her to force him to leave. To see the disgust in her gaze. To be sent away so he could die inside.

But now she stood there, hands outstretched, asking him to stay. Asking him to make free with her body and heart.

Offering him a gift he hadn't deserved but vowed to earn.

"You wish that of me? I who was scarce human when you met me? You could have any man you wished, lass. Any of the villagers. Nay, even Scotia's king."

"I want only you. Or no one. Ever."

"You would trust me so? To be your . . . man?"

"I trust you already."

Aedan stared at her. He began to speak several times, then closed his mouth again.

"If you refuse me, I'll cast myself into the sea," she announced dramatically. "And *die*." Not really, because Jane Sillee wasn't a quitter, but he needn't know that.

"Nay—you will not go to the sea!" he roared. Eyes glittering, he moved toward her.

"I am so lonely without you, Aedan," Jane said simply.

"You truly want me?"

"More than anything. I'm only half without you."

"Then you are my woman." His words were finality, a bond he would not permit broken. She had given herself to his keeping. He would never let her go.

"And you'll never leave me?" she pressed.

"I'll stay with you for all of ever, lass."

Jane's eyes flared, and she looked at him strangely. "And then yet another day?" she asked breathlessly.

"Oh, aye."

"And we could have babies?"

"Half dozen if you wish."

"Could we start making them now?"

"Oh, aye." A grin touched his lips; the first full grin she'd ever seen on his gorgeous face. The effect was devastating: It was a dangerous, knowing grin that dripped sensual promise. "I should warn you," he said, his eyes glittering, "I recall what it is to be a man now, lass. *All* of it. And I was ever a man of greedy and demanding appetites."

"Oh, please," Jane breathed. "Be as greedy as you wish. Demand away."

"I will begin small," he said, his eyes sparkling. "We will begin with the pressing of the lips you so favor," he teased.

Jane flung herself at him, and when his arms closed around her, she went wild, touching and kissing and clinging to him.

"Woman, I need you," he growled, slanting his mouth across hers. "Ever since I remembered the things a man knows, all I could think of were the things I ached to do to you."

"Show me," she whimpered.

And he did, taking his sweet time, peeling away her gown until she was naked before him, kissing and suckling and tasting every inch of her.

He experienced no difficulty whatsoever finding her most private heat.

Fifteen

THE UNSEELIE KING SENSED IT THE PRECISE MOMENT he lost his Vengeance. Though the mortal Highlander had not yet regained full memory, he loved and was loved in return.

The king's visage changed in a manner most rare for him; the corners of his lips turned up.

Humans, he thought mockingly, *so easily manipulated.* How infuriated they would be if they knew it had never been about them to begin with, and, indeed, rarely was. His Vengeance had performed precisely as he'd expected, twisting his three nebulous suggestions, and with obstinate human defiance, aiding the king in his aim.

Eons ago, a young Seelie queen for whom he suffered an unending hunger had escaped him before he'd been through with her.

She'd not risked entering his realm again.

His smile grew. If he must stoop to conquer, it was not beneath him.

He swallowed a laugh, tossed his head back, and let loose an enraged roar that resonated throughout the fabric of the universe.

The Seelie queen heard the dark king's cry and permitted herself a small, private smile.

So, she mused, feeling quite lovely, he had lost and she had won. It made her feel positively magnanimous. Sipping the nectar from a splendidly plump dalisonia, she rolled onto her back and stretched languidly.

Perhaps she should offer the dark king her condolences, she mused. After all, they were royalty, and royalty did that sort of thing.

After all, she had won.

She could simply duck in and back out, gloat a bit.

And if he tried to restrain her? Keep her captive in his realm? She laughed softly. She'd beaten him this time. She'd *proved* that she was stronger than she'd been millennia ago when he'd caged her for a time.

Feeling potent, inebriated on victory, she closed her eyes and envisioned his icy lair . . .

The iciness of his realm stole her breath away. Then she saw him and inhaled sharply, sucking in great lungfuls of icy air. Her memory had not done him justice. He was even more exotic than she'd recalled. A palpable darkness surrounded him. He was deadly and powerful, and she knew from intimate experience just how inventively, exhaustively erotic he was. A true master of pain, he understood pleasure as no other could.

"My queen," he said, his eyes of night and ice glittering.

Even as powerful as the Seelie queen was, she found it impossible to gaze into his eyes for more than a moment. Some claimed they'd been emptied of matter and pure chaos had been spooned into the sockets.

She inclined her head, averting her gaze ever so slightly. "It would seem you have lost your Vengeance, dark one," she murmured.

"It would seem I have."

When he rose from his throne of ice, and rose and rose, she caught her breath. Not quite faery, his blood mixed with the blood of a creature even the Fae hesitated to name. His shadow moved unnaturally as he rose, slithering around him, wont to move independently of its host.

"You seem unperturbed by your defeat, dark one," she probed, determined to savor every drop of her victory. "Care you not that you have lost him? Five centuries of work. Wasted."

"You presume you knew my aim."

The Seelie queen stiffened, staring into his eyes for a moment longer than was wise. "Pretend not that you intended to lose. That I have been manipulated." Her voice dripped ice worthy of his kingdom.

"Loss is a relative thing."

"I won. *Admit* it," she snapped.

"I doubt you even knew what game we played, young one." His voice deep, silky, and mesmerizing, he mocked, "Did you come to gloat because my defeat made you feel powerful? Did it make you feel safe in seeking me? Careful. A being such as I might be inclined to find you reason to condescend. To sink to my depths."

"I have sunk to nothing," she hissed, feeling suddenly foolish. She *was* young by his standards, for the king of darkness was ancient—sprung from the loins of an age she'd heard of only in legend.

He said nothing, merely regarded her, his stare a palpable weight. She repressed a shiver, remembering her last excursion to his land. She'd nearly failed to summon the power to leave. But, she conceded with a thrill of sexual anticipation so intense that it nearly brought her to her knees, she'd not quite been in a hurry to leave the dark king's dangerous bed. And therein lay double the danger . . .

"I came to offer my condolences," she said coolly.

His laughter alone could seduce. "So offer, my queen." He moved in a swirl of darkness. "But offer that for which we both know you hunger. Your willing surrender."

And when he was upon her, when he had gathered her up and his great wings began to flap, she let her head fall against his icy breast. Darkness so thick that it had texture and taste surrounded her. "Never."

"Heed me well, light one, the only thing you are never with me—is safe."

Much later, when he possessed her completely, a full blood moon stained the sky above the Highlands of Scotland.

Aedan made love to Jane like a man who understood that this day, this moment, only this *now* was securely in the palm of his hand, taking her with the passionate urgency of a tenth-century Scotsman who knew not what tomorrow might bring: brutal war, drought, or crop-destroying tempest. He made love like a drowning man, desperate for the surety of her body—she was his shore, his raft, his harbor against what storms may come.

And then he made love to her again.

This time, with exquisite gentleness. Brushed his lips against the warm hollow of her neck in which her heartbeat pulsed. Kissed the slopes of her breasts, tasted the salt of her skin and the sweetness of her passion glistening between her thighs, and flexed himself deep within her innermost warmth.

He became part of her. Finally, he knew the kind of loving that made two one and understood Jane was his world. His ocean, his country, his sun, his rain, his very heart.

And that sleek, iced citadel behind his breastbone— behind which he'd concealed from the dark king that which was most infinitely precious to him—cracked at the foundations and came crashing down.

And he finally remembered what he'd sealed away there . . . his Jane.

"Jane, my own sweet Jane," he cried hoarsely.

Jane's eyes flew wide. He was buried deep within her, loving her slowly and intensely, and although he'd called her name aloud many times during the loving, his voice sounded different this time.

Could it be he'd finally remembered all of it? All those years they'd spent together in dreams, playing and loving and dancing and loving?

"Aedan?" His name held the question she was afraid to ask.

Framing her head with his forearms, he stared down at her. "You came to me. I remember now. You came when I slept. In the Dreaming."

"Yes," Jane cried, joyous tears misting her eyes.

There were no words for a time, only the soft sounds of passion, of a woman being thoroughly loved by her man.

When finally she could catch her breath again, she said, "You were with me always. You watched me grow up, remember?" She laughed self-consciously. "When I was thirteen, I nearly dreaded seeing you because I was so gawky—"

"Nay, you were no such thing. You were a wee lovely lass, I watched your womanhood ripening and saw what you would become. I ached for the day you would be old enough that I could love you in every way."

"Well, you didn't have to wait *quite* so long," she voiced a long-harbored complaint. *"Mmm,"* she added, gasping, when he nipped her nipple lightly with his teeth. "Do that again."

He did. And again, until her breasts felt ripe and exquisitely sensitive. Then he rubbed his unshaven cheek lightly against her peaked nipples, creating delicious friction.

"I claimed you when you were ten and eight," he managed finally.

"Like I said—long. I was ready way before then. I was ready by sixteen . . . *Ooh!"*

"You were a wee babe still," he said indignantly, stilling inside her.

"Don't stop," she gasped.

"Doona think for a minute 'twasn't difficult for me to naysay you. 'Twas that my mother insisted all her sons forgo impatience and give a lass time to be a child before having bairn of her own."

"Please," she whimpered.

Heeding her plea, he thrust without cease, and she cried out his name over and again, digging her fingers into his muscular hips, pulling him as deep as she could take him.

He kissed her, taking her cries with his lips until her shudders subsided.

"Have you had time enough, wee Jane?" he asked later, when she lay drowsy and sated in his arms. "We may have made one this very day, you ken."

Jane beamed. His shimmering eyes were again a warm tropical surf in his dark face, his lips curved with sensuality and tenderness. He'd finally remembered her! And she might have his baby growing inside her. "I want half a dozen at least," she assured him, smiling.

Then she sobered, touching his jaw lightly. "When I was twenty-two, the dreams seemed different. They became repeats of earlier dreams."

His jaw tensed beneath her hand.

"I lost you," she said. "Didn't I?"

"The king discovered I was gaining strength from my dreams. He prevented me from joining you there," Aedan said tersely.

She inhaled sharply. "How?" she asked, not certain she wanted to know.

"You doona wish to know, and I doona need to speak of it. 'Tis over and done," he said, his eyes darkening.

Jane didn't press, and let it go, for now, knowing the time would come when he would need to speak of it, and she would be there to listen. For now, she would wait while Aedan became fully Aedan again.

He smiled suddenly, dazzling her. "You were my light, wee Jane. My laughter, my hope, my love, and now you will be my wife."

"Ahem," she said pertly, "if you think you're getting off with that lame proposal, you have another thought coming."

He laughed. "Your headstrong nature was one of the first things I favored in you, lass. So much fire, and as cold as I was, your tempers kept me warm. Saucy like my mother, demanding like my sisters, yet tender of heart and weak of will when it comes to passion."

"Who are you calling weak?" she said, with mock indignation.

Aedan gave her a provocative glance from beneath half-lowered lids. "'Tis obvious you have a weakness for me. You spent the past fortnight trying to seduce me—"

"Only because you'd forgotten me! Otherwise *you* would have been chasing *me* around!"

Certain of it, she scrambled from beneath him and slipped from the bed, then dashed out into the great hall. Sure enough, he followed, stalking her like a great greedy dark beast.

And when he caught her . . .

And when he caught her, he made wild, passionate love to her. Celestial music trumpeted from the heavens. (It did. I swear.) Rainbows gathered to shimmer above Dun Haa-

kon. Heather bloomed, and even the sun's brilliance paled in comparison to the luminosity of true love.

And when he proposed again, it was on bended knee, with a band of gold embedded with tiny heart-shaped rubies, as he vowed to love her for all of ever. Then yet another day.

—From the unpublished manuscript
Highland Fire by Jane MacKinnon

Epilogue

"Don't forget the latest chapter, Aedan," Jane reminded as he slipped from their bed. "I missed last week, and Henna said they're going to storm the castle if I don't let them know what's going on with Beth and Duncan."

"I won't forget, lass." Donning shirt and plaid, Aedan picked up the parchments from the sidetable. He glanced at the top page.

She held her breath, waiting for him to kiss her, knowing that she would never be the same once she'd tasted the passion of his embrace. Her braw Highlander had fought valiantly for the Bruce and had come home to her wounded in body and heart. But she would heal him . . .

"You know, the men say that since their wives have been reading your tales they're much more . . . er, amorous,"

Aedan told her. Downright bawdy, the men had actually said. Insatiable. Plotting ways to seduce their men at all hours. Her stories had the same effect on him. Reading one of her love scenes never failed to make him hard as a rock. He wondered if she suspected that before delivering her pages to the eager women, he stopped in the tavern where the husbands listened, with much jesting and guffawing, as he read the most recent installment. Although they made sport of the "mushy parts," not one of them failed to show each Tuesday when he made his weekly trip to the village. Last week, three of them had come looking for *him* when he'd failed to appear with that week's installment.

"Really?" Jane was delighted.

"Aye," he said, grinning. "They thank you for it."

Jane beamed. As he pulled on his boots, she reminded him, "Oh, and don't forget, I want peach ice, not blueberry."

"I willna forget," he promised. "You've got the entire village making your favored dish. I vow when the spring thaws come and they can't make your icy cream they may go mad."

Jane smiled. She'd been unable to resist teaching the villagers a few things that she deemed reasonably harmless. It wasn't like she was advancing technology before its time. Pushing the drapes aside, she glanced out the window behind the bed. "It snowed again last night. Look—isn't it beautiful, Aedan?" she exclaimed.

Aedan pulled the drapes back over the window and tucked the covers more securely around her. "Aye, 'tis lovely. And damned cold. Are you warm enough?" he worried. Without waiting for her reply, he stacked several more logs on the fire and banked it carefully. "I doona want you getting out of bed. You mustn't catch a chill."

Jane made a face. "I'm not *that* pregnant, Aedan. I still have two more months."

"I willna take any chances with you or our daughter."

"Son."

"Daughter."

Jane's laughter was cut off abruptly when he took her in his arms and kissed her long and hard before leaving.

At the doorway he paused. "If 'tis a lass," he asked softly, "do you think we might name her Rose?"

"Oh, yes, Aedan," Jane said softly. "I'd like that."

After he left, Jane lay back against the pillows, marveling. Seven months had passed since her arrival at Dun Haakon, and although there'd been some difficult moments, she wouldn't have traded it for anything in the world.

Aedan still had a great deal of darkness inside him, of times and things he rarely discussed. There had been somber months while he'd grieved the loss of his clan. Then finally, one morning she'd come down from their new bedchamber above-stairs and found him hanging the old portraits in the great hall. She'd watched him, praying he wouldn't have that stark expression in his eyes. When he'd raised his head and smiled at her, her heart had soared.

"'Tis time to honor the past," he'd told her. "We have a rich history, lass. I want our children to know their grandparents."

Then he'd made love to her, there in the great hall. They'd rolled across the floor, paused for a heated interlude on the table, and ended up, she recalled, blushing, in a most interesting position over a chair.

All of her dreams had come true. The village women waited with bated breath for the latest "installment" of her serial novel. They lapped up every word, savoring the romance, and the magic of it spilled over into their hearth and home. And no one ever complained about purple prose or typos.

She was a storyteller with an eager audience, a mother-to-be, had a milking cow of her own, reasonably hot water, the scent of her man all over her skin, and she slept each night held tightly in the arms of the man she loved.

Dreamily, she sighed, resting her hand on her tummy. Sexpot gave a little pink-tongued yawn and snuggled closer beside her.

Life was *good*.

AUTHOR'S NOTE

MY YOUNGER SISTER HAS LONG ENTERTAINED ME WITH SILLY Jane Jokes. What is a Silly Jane Joke? Elizabeth is so glad you asked!

A carpenter asked the very curvaceous Silly Jane to help him. He'd hurt his foot and needed someone to climb up the ladder and retrieve his bucket of paint from the top. But Silly Jane was no fool. She knew that he just wanted to look up her dress and see her panties when she climbed it. So she tricked him. She took her panties off first.

This story is a work of fiction. Any resemblance between Silly Jane and Jane Sillee is purely coincidental. Really.

AFTERWORD

SINCE JANE SILLEE IS AN ASPIRING WRITER AND FOLKS HAVE expressed an interest in my path to publication, this seems the perfect place to share a bit. For those of you, like Jane, who are struggling to find your audience in the current state of the publishing world, I hope that what I'm about to tell you inspires you to stay the course, no matter how tough it gets. In today's market it's possible that the pressure to write what sells and forget about your heart has never been more intense.

Rule number one about writing: All the best stories come from the heart.

Back in 1998 when my agent was trying to sell *Beyond the Highland Mist,* the publishing industry was categorically rejecting paranormal romance. The hot ticket was straight historical, emphasis on Regency. I'd been trying to get published, off and on, for several years and I seemed to keep missing whatever boat was currently leaving the dock. Some days I wasn't even sure I was on the right dock. Or on a dock at all.

One of my earliest novels (written in 1993–94) was about the clan Douglas, and plotted around the story of Robert the Bruce. Every agent and publisher I submitted to told me that no one wanted to read a story about that time period or those "primitive Highlanders." They said it would never get published and I should focus on Regency. I gave up on my novel, and exactly one year later *Braveheart* was released in theaters, followed by *Rob Roy*.

My next unpublished novel, *The Lady Lies,* was a sizzling, non-paranormal Regency that publishers told me was simply too sexy. Is there any such thing today?

With my Scots too primitive, and my Regencies too sexy, I decided to try something new but I wasn't sure what. I'd written several novels by that time and had accumulated the requisite stack of rejection letters. They never bothered me because I figured they were rungs in a ladder and eventually, if I had the perseverance to keep climbing, I'd get to the top. At least they were proof that I was *on* the ladder. Then one day I got a rejection letter that said my storytelling was excellent, my writing was good, but it wasn't commercial enough. I mulled it over for days. I think that was the first time I truly realized that writing was a business and if I wanted to support myself doing it, I needed to reevaluate what I was writing and make it more sellable.

Thus resolved, when I began my next book, I made sure it had too much sex *and* primitive Highlanders *and* time travel and, if that wasn't enough to abso-frigging-lutely guarantee rejection, I upped the ante and tossed in the Fae. I have no idea what I was thinking. I knew better. I knew it was going to get rejected, but I was having so much fun writing that I didn't care. It was the story I wanted to tell. It might not have been the right dock, but it was *my* dock.

When Random House made an offer for it, I was flabbergasted. When they made it a two-book deal, I thought I'd died and gone to heaven. I still have the napkin I wrote the deal notes on. I was sitting in a cubicle at Great American Insurance Company, eating a late lunch when I got the call. Tuna salad, chips, and a dill pickle. I've forgotten no details of that momentous day.

Looking back, I'm staggered that Maggie Crawford—thank you, Maggie!—took the chance on *Beyond the Highland Mist*. It was far too paranormal, far too out there, considering what was and wasn't selling at the time. I was encouraged to write a straight historical for the next novel, which I did.

By the time my second novel was finished, *Beyond the Highland Mist* had been released and sold very well, astounding most of us, and giving me a track record to look at going into my third book. I actually earned royalties on my first royalty statement, which was unheard of in the genre back then. It received numerous awards, was nominated for two RITAs, and I took home a plaque for Waldenbooks Bestselling Debut Romance Author of 1999.

Fortified by the success of my time-traveling Fae novel, I submitted a third paranormal proposal called *Ghost of a Chance,* included in this compilation, that tells the unpublished story of Hawk Douglas's brother, Adrian. It was turned down, and I was advised once again to focus on straight historical. Paranormal was the smallest dock in the market, and publishers just didn't want to take a chance on it.

I wrote *The Highlander's Touch* next and set it during the time of Robert the Bruce. (I may get detoured but I never stop trying to turn down the same street.) In my proposal, I downplayed the elements of time travel and Fae. In the book, I gave them free reign. I didn't exactly mean to, I just couldn't help myself.

Then something happened that changed everything. My editor left and took a different job while I was writing *The Highlander's Touch,* and for some reason no one made me eliminate the paranormal elements, and my next proposal was quickly approved.

By this time in my career, I was beginning to think I was on to something with my time-travel/Fae world. My second toned-down novel hadn't done well at all. No strong criticism. No strong compliments. Tepid is the word that comes to mind. I'd rather be strongly rejected than tepidly received. My third highly paranormal novel won a RITA.

With my newfound freedom, I decided to continue with the time-travel/Fae combination and develop the mythology further with twin druids whose clan had served the Fae for millennia. It was while writing those novels that my voice became very clear to me, and I began to develop a mythology I found fascinating and had a blast writing. Rule number two in the writing world: If the writer is having fun, the reader probably will, too.

When I took a short break between *Kiss of the Highlander* and *The Dark Highlander* to write *Into the Dreaming* for a different publisher, I could feel myself chafing at the way the confines of the genre were limiting the story I wanted to tell. I was becoming increasingly aware that I was skimming the surface, always pulling back whenever the waters started to get deep and dark—which to me is exactly when things get interesting. Over and over, I caught myself pulling my punches, muscling the story line, not letting it go where it wanted to go. My muse was getting more and more miserable and so was I.

What I didn't realize was that I was dying to write urban fantasy—but the genre didn't exist yet. It was still being spawned by writers with stories to tell that didn't fit in any single genre, and by readers like you, who'd been waiting impatiently for the stories to get a little darker and deeper.

Fans have been asking me for years how *Into the Dreaming* fits into the overall scheme of my novels and world-building because the parallels with the Fever series are unmistakable—a dark Unseelie king in an icy fortress, a beautiful Seelie queen, an ancient war, an eternal love affair, the Song of Making—yet it was written long before I began *Darkfever*. *Into the Dreaming* was the birth pains of the Fever world. I was having them even then. But my romance novels were too successful, and the money too good to try to fix something that wasn't broken.

I wrote three more Highlander novels after *Into the Dreaming: The Dark Highlander, The Immortal Highlander,* and *Spell of the Highlander.* When I finished *Spell* in 2004, I was more exhausted than I'd ever been after completing a book. Though I loved the characters and the story, I'd had to force myself to finish it. I needed to write grittier, darker books. It was where my heart was.

But my publisher wanted my proposal for my next *romance* novel.

I stalled.

They emailed and said, Where is it?

My computer died.

They called.

Cell signal encountered technical difficulties reaching my house.

They threatened to visit.

I moved.

That's when I had the dream in which I got the entire story of the Fever series, all five books in one night, complete with all the characters, plot, even the installment breaks. Looking back, I see the culmination of years of repression. The stories were there, waiting to be told. They wanted to come out. It's the pattern of my life: I get detoured, but eventually I'm going to turn down that one-way street with all those potholes that's blocked off. May as well just move the barricades out of the way. I *like* the dark, less-traveled, road.

It's funny to me how things come full circle. I began my writing career with the Fae, when everyone and everything around me—except you, my dear reader—was warning me to give up the paranormal, get serious, and write straight romance novels. Yet, looking back over my career, the one novel that was closest to being a straight romance novel has sold less to date than any other book I've written. I've learned many important things during my writing career but here's the golden rule for aspiring writers: Trust your gut and trust your readers. Respect them both and they won't steer you wrong. Don't waste your time trying to find the "right" dock. Spend that time making *your* dock the best it can be.

Each time I've taken a risk, dear reader, you were right there, taking it with me. When I moved from romance to urban fantasy, most of you made the jump. Some of you didn't and hope that I'll eventually return to my romance roots. I can't say that I have any plans to do that right now, but I've shared some pieces in this collection just for you.

I can't thank you enough. None of this would have been possible without you. You followed when I jumped, you kept the faith when it got dark, and stayed to the lights on my promise alone that it would be worth it. (My books come with unique catchphrases. I don't choose them. They present themselves in theme and repetition. For the Fever series it was "stay to the lights.")

Iced comes out in October, the first book in my new Dani O'Malley trilogy. I'm jumping again. Some people are worried and think maybe I should stay on the safe dock, the one that the boats have been going to for the last five books of Mac and Barrons's series. But when I get up in the morning, grab my coffee, and sit down at the computer, all I can hear is Dani O'Malley talking. It's her turn now, and her voice has never been clearer.

She's saying: Never. Going. To. Happen.

Karen

I wrote this in 1999. Looking back, I see what a rough proposal it was and the many things I should have changed or developed further. Still, after all these years, I think it would have been a great story!

GHOST OF A CHANCE

When twenty-eight-year-old Dr. Penelope Jonté decides to begin a new life, she purchases a magnificent castle nestled above the sleepy village of Ballyhock, Scotland. She never dreams that the ancient and opulent legacy of Lyssford-at-the-Lea comes with a five-hundred-year-old Scottish warrior, cursed with immortality.

Central Characters

Dr. Penelope Jonté: heroine, twenty-eight-year-old doctor of psychology. She has an IQ of 165 and was a child prodigy. She graduated early, and after several of her publications received national acclaim, she was offered an extremely lucrative position in Cincinnati as exclusive staff psychologist for Interon, Inc., a prestigious engineering and research firm. There she counseled the overly bright, often-inarticulate, troubled employees. She is five feet eight inches, with a sleek fall of hair and dark eyes. Her mother is dead, and she has never known her father.

Adrian Bruce Douglas the Black: hero, Hawk Douglas's brother, cursed to inhabit Lyssford forever. He is invisible, immortal, and cannot leave the estate. He resembles the Douglas Norse ancestors: six feet four inches, he has blond hair, light green eyes, and golden skin—if one could see him. He can touch, but if someone runs into him he can be walked through, unless his intent to touch is present.

Brunhilde: a Valkyrie endowed with special powers, the witch who curses Adrian.

Dinah Bancroft: secondary romance heroine. She ran away from home in America at seventeen with her high school history teacher (who should be shot). They were going to backpack around Europe, but when he discovered she was pregnant, he abandoned her in Scotland. She got a job as a waitress and miscarried the baby. She is stunning and has very large breasts, which are difficult to ignore. Men have always treated her only as an object and she has no sense of self-worth as anything other than a sexual companion. She longs to be loved for something besides her appearance. Two months prior to Penelope's arrival, she caught mono and was unable to work (she has no health insurance). She stowed away in the carriage house at Lyssford and has barely been hanging on. Her character will demonstrate several things: healing the doctor in Penelope who comes to Lyssford afraid to counsel again, and falling in love with a blind man who finally "sees" her as she really is.

Jamie McIntyre: secondary romance hero. Twenty-seven-year-old, blind gardener at Lyssford. He is also the local attorney. He graduated from law school and returned to his hometown. Since he has a knack with flowers and plants, and there's not much legal business in the tiny village of Bally-hock, he is happy to take the post at Lyssford, handling his practice in the evening.

Jenkyn Gilchrist: Lyssford's eclectic butler, obsessed with the derivation of language.

Lizzy Gilchrist: Lyssford's housekeeper, and Jenkyn's wife. Both late bloomers and somewhat homely, they are deliriously in love and quibble happily over vocabulary while playing a nightly game of Scrabble in the kitchen. Penelope finds that more genuine, positive counseling takes place over their game board than in any office she's been in. She draws up a chair in the kitchen more than once, as do most of the characters.

SYNOPSIS

Ghost of a Chance opens with a prologue set at Dalkeith-Upon-the-Sea. Hawk Douglas and his wife, Adrienne, are hosting a costume ball to celebrate both Beltane and Adrian Douglas's thirtieth birthday. The hero is a dissolute womanizer and Hawk has determined that what he needs to mature is a little responsibility. As a birthday present, he bequeaths the title to Lyssford to his younger brother, who in a drunken bout of honesty informs him he'd rather take a vow of celibacy than live on that godforsaken moor.

Adrian encounters a stunning woman at the ball, clad in Viking costume, and slips off to make love with her in the gardens. When he behaves insufferably, she curses him. Adrian is unaware that he has just mortally offended Brunhilde, mightiest of the Valkyries. The curse she lays upon him is that he is condemned to live forever at Lyssford (since she heard him say he'd rather take a vow of celibacy than live there), confined by its perimeters and invisible (unable to exploit women by using his incredible looks) until he proves himself worthy of a woman's love.

[Author's note: The following information regarding Adrian and the terms of his enchantment will be presented throughout the story via dialogue with the heroine and Adrian's reflections. It will be interspersed through the story, not dumped like this, but I suspect you may have many questions that can best be answered by fully explaining Adrian to you at the onset of the proposal.]

Adrian doesn't hear Brunhilde's curse, and doesn't know the terms of it.

He simply disappears, then is suddenly at Lyssford, invisible, with no idea what transpired. He can't see himself. He casts no reflection in a mirror. People can walk through him, but he can touch if he intends to touch. He can speak, hear, and all his senses are intact, but if he ever tries to discuss what happened to him, how he came to be the invisible, immortal prisoner of Lyssford, a rush of words come out of his mouth that are mortifying. *"I am an arrogant, insensitive, lack-witted blackguard, who doesn't deserve a woman's love—and I'm lousy in bed to boot."*

131

(Brunhilde has a twisted sense of humor. She figures that if he ever is smart enough to realize what the curse is, he'll deter any woman who might consider absolving him with those words. It's quite comical the first time he answers Penelope's questions.)

At odd intervals over the centuries, he seems to grow more substantial, for no reason that he can discern. Once he could even see the outline of his hands, and a foggy reflection of himself in the glass, but those times were short-lived and he swiftly became completely invisible again. (Although he doesn't know it—because he doesn't know he was cursed—Brunhilde's curse lasts only a number of years, so she must come to renew it. In this manner she checks on him, to verify for her own pleasure that he is still not free.)

During the early years of his confinement he suffers extreme isolation. Hawk and Adrienne, so distraught by his disappearance and apparent death, seal Lyssford, and seventy-five years pass before anyone ever comes again. Unremitting, relentless solitude. Adrian does not need to eat, although he can, and enjoys it tremendously.

Various tenants occupy the estate over five centuries. Initially, Adrian tries to communicate and meets with disastrous results. If he doesn't terrify the occupants, they think he is a druid spirit or a sorcerer and try to use him for gain. In the 1700s, he is drawn to an occupant's children and plays with them. Initially the parents believe their children have an imaginary friend, but eventually they fear that their children are being beguiled by a demon, so they bring a priest to perform an exorcism. At first Adrian finds it amusing, until he feels something terrible happening to him and flees the house in panic, racing to the farthest perimeter of the estate. He has learned his lesson, and never again attempts to communicate after that. He knows he can't die, but the near-exorcism convinces him that there might be worse things than his present condition.

In time, he savors having tenants in "his" castle because they bring new inventions, new ideas. During a vacancy of twenty-five years in the 1800s he thought he would go mad from the solitude. He can't leave the estate. If he ventures past its perimeters, he endures excruciating pain, as if he is coming apart cell by cell. Once he nearly strayed too far, and now he believes that if he ever did again, he would simply cease to exist.

During the sixty years preceding Penelope's occupancy, a childless couple, who loved with such a tender, selfless love that it rocked Adrian to his very soul, occupied Lyssford. Adrian never attempted communication with them, but he did leave little gifts and do small favors, making their lives easier in countless ways. Nothing ever broke in their castle (or if it did, it was repaired late at night by a benevolent handyman who charged no fee). Five hundred years later, Adrian the Black is a very different man.

Eight years of vacancy ensue after the childless couple dies and his precious companions—the TV, the CDs, and the books—are outdated and on the verge of breaking. The TV dies the day the latest owner, Dr. Jonté, arrives. The moment Adrian sees her, he is hopelessly drawn to her. He has been growing stronger again. The time seems rife with possibilities, and after studying Penelope and snooping through her computer files, he quickly concludes that the odds for communication with her are high—and relatively without risk. She is pragmatic, compassionate, and intelligent (almost as smart as him, he decides, although she hasn't had the benefit of five hundred years of study).

He finds her impossibly alluring and quickly rationalizes contact.

Penelope is initially frightened by the "ghost," but progresses through the stages of denial, fear, and anger, evolving slowly to incredulous belief. His unremitting tenderness and understanding woo her, despite her logical mind's objection to his existence.

As he and Penelope grow intimate, she tries to understand how he came to be what he is. He can't talk about it, but he can talk about his life before the curse. Later in the story, he directs her to Dalkeith, to search for information about what happened to him. At Dalkeith, she uncovers old diaries and personal effects and they start to piece together Adrian's story. It is also there that she sees the first portrait of her invisible lover—and he is magnificent.

The middle of the book is devoted to the increasing closeness between Penelope and her "ghost," with a secondary romance between Dinah and her blind gardener. With proper food and care, Dinah makes a rapid recovery and slowly she and Penelope become friends. Penelope bargains with her, offering the girl employment in her home on the condition that Dinah attends a nearby university and pursues an education. Dinah, growing close to the gardener, and stunned by her discovery that the man she initially pitied for his blindness is a lawyer, agrees. (She also makes the error of thinking that since he's blind he must be a virgin—so many misconceptions, much like the ones made about her. Large breasts =

bimbo?) Dinah begins to blossom and gets involved with her new classes. She starts out slowly, taking just two classes, and works at the castle for her keep and education. Her progress is hard-won and delightful.

Penelope's motivation for nurturing Dinah is rooted in her recent professional and personal catastrophe. As staff psychologist for Interon, Inc., Dr. Jonté treated the firm's brilliant, neurotic, and often-inarticulate employees. She counseled only adults, until an engineer she was particularly fond of begged her to work with his extremely bright daughter. Reluctantly, she accepted the case, but met with failure for the first time in her career. The adolescent girl committed suicide.

Suddenly, Penelope found herself challenging everything she believed in. She had tried all the classic textbook things, as well as more unconventional psychology with the child. She talked and listened, and exercised every ounce of her *superior* intellect—and still failed.

Distraught by her failure that cost a child's life, she left Interon, Inc., and secluded herself for months on end trying to pinpoint where she went wrong. During those months, desperate for a distraction from her depression, she played with her portfolio, riding waves via the Internet. Angered by the inability of her "brilliant mind" to save a little girl's life, she devoted her massive IQ to turning her already reasonable fortune into an incredible one.

But Interon wouldn't leave her alone. The engineers were bitterly complaining that their doctor had abandoned them. Interon went through several replacements with no success, and tried to tempt Dr. Jonté to return, initially with a generous offer, but finally with thinly veiled threats about exposing her "failure" publicly and humiliating her.

Determined never to return to Interon or counseling, she left the country and traveled, then bought Lyssford, drawn by an inexplicable sense of belonging.

At Lyssford, Penelope learns to love life again, falls in love with her ghost, and learns to forgive herself.

Lyssford is a haven for a group of unusual people. They bond to one another, each character a bit odd, and perhaps for that reason, are more tolerant and sensitive than the average person. At one point, Dinah, who is slowly thawing, posts a sign on the outside of the castle that says, "Welcome to the Land of Misfit Toys." When Penelope sees it, she laughs just like Julia Roberts in *Pretty Woman*.

Penelope and Adrian grow closer, and share much of their lives with one another.

Late at night, Adrian does research, gets on the computer, and delves into records. He discovers that the child Penelope couldn't save had ADD, and that her parents, both brilliant engineers, refused to allow her to take medication and drilled it into their daughter's head that if she had a problem concentrating, it was her fault, her failure to properly focus, her lack of discipline. They never told Penelope that their daughter had ADD. So the child was fighting ADD and, believing it was her problem, was too ashamed to admit to Penelope that she had it. Penelope is astonished and saddened when she learns this, and slowly starts to forgive herself.

As indicated earlier, Adrian is growing stronger (the

curse is wearing down and Brunhilde is due for a visit). He fully manifests and Penelope finally sees him for the first time. He is splendid. He has no idea why he can be seen, but they both suspect he may finally be free of whatever was wrong. She is elated. They make love for the first time with him visible, and it is incredible. Penelope introduces her friend to the staff (although no one is really fooled).

Some weeks later, Penelope goes to meet Dinah at the university for a previously arranged meeting. It is a stormy day, with heavy rains and flash flooding in and around the valley that nestles Ballyhock.

When Penelope and Dinah don't return by late evening, Adrian and the Gilchrists are frantic. They call a cab to go look for them, but the cabs aren't running because the weather is so bad. Adrian takes off on foot into the storm. He goes down the valley, through the woods, to the edge of the property and crosses it, drawn by the beacon of headlights pointing skyward, and as he nears, he hears the sound of Dinah's cries. He finds her with Penelope; a small flash flood had washed them over a slab and Penelope has been knocked unconscious.

As Adrian kneels beside Penelope, he starts to feel himself coming apart. He carries her back toward Lyssford, but he has been too long off the estate and is dissipating. When he gets her close to the house, she regains consciousness and sees that he is fading.

Suddenly, he disappears.

———

Adrian materializes in a hut in the woods. He has no idea where he is or what time it is. He is about to march out the door, when Brunhilde flings it open, all seductive woman, trying to seduce him (some people *never* change, and Adrian accuses her of failing to evolve when *he* did so splendidly). Pieces start to fall into place and make sense to Adrian. They fight and she finally tells him what she did to him and why. But now that he has offered his life for the love of a woman (knowing he would cease to exist, he still rescued Penelope), he is free of the curse and may return to Dalkeith and his own time.

Adrian is outraged and argues eloquently to be returned to the woman whose love freed him. Petulantly, Brunhilde refuses. Adrian demands a fair trial and Brunhilde, her interest piqued by this possibility, grants him a hearing before her sister Valkyries. He argues his case—his love for Penelope—before the full tribunal of Valkyries. (One man, convincing nine women of his love for Penelope—great scene!)

They vote to return him to his woman. Even Brunhilde is swayed. But Adrian wants his life back. He demands to be given the choice of staying with her or having Penelope return with him. (Throughout the story, Penelope has expressed a longing to live in a simpler time, when she wouldn't have been considered brilliant, because most people didn't read and write. He wants to be able to give her the choice.)

Brunhilde grudgingly concedes to leave it up to Penelope.

The story concludes precisely where it began: at the masked ball at Dalkeith-Upon-the-Sea. Adrienne and Hawk are frantically looking for Adrian, who disappeared a few hours before.

Suddenly, he comes strolling in with a beautiful, oddly

garbed woman (who certainly piques Adrienne's interest) and four strangers. He apologizes to Adrienne and Hawk and says it is definitely time he settled down—he's wasted a *lot* of years, so he will marry this woman and gratefully accept their birthday gift—and this is his new staff, by the way.

———

The last page is a newspaper clipping:

The entire staff of Lyssford-at-the-Lea seemingly vanished overnight. The oddest thing is that they seem to have hung new portraits right before they vanished . . .

KISS OF THE HIGHLANDER

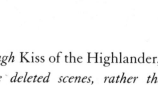

Halfway through Kiss of the Highlander, *I took a wrong turn. In these deleted scenes, rather than confronting Drustan with the truth, Gwen claims amnesia—and nearly has sex with the laird of the castle up against the wall in a corridor shortly after arriving! In this version, she doesn't get confronted by both Dageus and Drustan the first morning she's there, and still believes Dageus is dead.*

CHAPTER 12

Silvan might be charming, Gwen mused, as she finally escaped from his clutches a few hours later, but he was also dangerous. Behind his disarming manners and haphazard gait lurked a clever, clever mind.

He'd nearly tripped her up a dozen times, and she'd had to resort to acting helpless and tiny and vulnerable. She'd even squeezed out a few tears during his subtle interrogation, and still she wasn't certain she'd convinced him that she recalled nothing of her life before this morning.

Thank God for Nell, who'd brought breakfast to Silvan's tower—soft poached eggs, deliciously salty ham, and crusty bread—and berated Silvan for pushing "the wee lass too hard and too soon, and canna ye see she has no memory?" Fierce, protective Nell, standing up to Silvan, bristling with indignation. In Gwen's estimation, Nell was what every mother should be.

And Silvan? He looked like a cross between a mad philosopher and a sorcerer in his brilliant blue robe, and had the instincts of a killer shark when he felt like exerting himself. Part of what threw Gwen off balance about Silvan was that he really *did* resemble Albert Einstein, and revering Einstein's work as she did, a bit of that adulation spilled over to Silvan, whether he deserved it or not.

But she'd quickly realized that his resemblance to the brilliant theorist didn't end with his appearance. She'd glimpsed a copy of Copernicus's *The Revolution of Heavenly Orbs* lying near his armchair. It had astonished her that a medieval man had a copy of the very recently published—1543, if her memory served her, and it always did—manuscript that had infuriated the Catholic Church with its claim that the earth orbited the sun, not vice versa.

He was as intriguing as his son, who knew how to manipulate time. Who were these men? And why did history mention nothing of them? If men had existed in the sixteenth century who knew so much about science, surely they would have penned at least one or two texts that survived to modern day.

Obviously, they were men of great intellect, who had a

heightened understanding of cosmology. Drustan possessed knowledge that had allowed him to access multidimensional travel. It was no wonder someone was after them. In her century, men would wipe out entire nations trying to get their hands on such knowledge.

Perplexed by the situation in which she found herself, she descended the stairs then paused at the bottom, pinching her lower lip and thinking.

I know it's 1545, Gwen had said in a disgustingly breathy, helpless voice to Silvan, hoping she had the year right, *but I can't seem to recall the month and day.*

He'd regarded her intently before telling her it was February twenty-fifth and not correcting her on the year, hence confirming its accuracy with his silence. She had one month to uncover the traitor.

She would create a list of the occupants of the castle, identify their place in the scheme of things, and determine who might have possible motive. Her primary goal was to prevent Drustan from being enchanted. Any scientific knowledge she might acquire would have to come second. Mentally, she'd begun to prepare a list of questions. She hoped that by the end of Silvan's interrogation she'd succeed in making him believe her a bit daft. No one expected too much of a simple-witted person, therefore no question she would ask might seem too strange.

"Lost, English?" a deep, mocking voice inquired, as the door to the Greathall slammed shut.

Gwen pressed her fingertips to her throat, shivering. He must have been standing in the doorway, watching her for several moments, perhaps the entire time she'd walked down the stairs, for she hadn't heard the door open.

When she'd found him in the cave, he'd called her English in exactly the same tone. *But he still doesn't know me,* she reminded herself. *Try not to let it hurt.* Pasting a smile on her lips she turned toward him. "It's a big castle. I'm still trying to find my way about."

God, he was gorgeous. Now that she knew he was truly a sixteenth-century lord, she wondered how she could have ever believed otherwise. He dripped command and control, as blatantly as he wore his sexuality. He was a man who thoroughly enjoyed being a man.

Looking grim, Drustan moved away from the door·and stalked in her direction.

Stalked.

Like a large, hungry, and very angry animal, his soft boots ate up the space between them. Dark, wild hair dusted with snow, body bristling with irritation, he cornered her.

It took all her willpower to not blurt a hasty apology for him having been accused of raping her. But since she'd told both Nell and Silvan that she could remember nothing but her own name, she could hardly exonerate him now.

"We need to talk," he growled, taking her by the elbow, steering her through the Greathall and propelling her down a corridor.

"Where are you taking me?" she asked, her toes barely skimming the floor. This, too, was similar to what he'd done in her time—wrapped a hand around her arm and dragged her through the tunnels. But there, he'd tried to seduce her first.

One could always hope.

"While you filled my da's head with more of your lies, I paid a visit to the village. It seems no one there is missing a wench. Or not one they're willing to own up to. Mayhap someone was glad to be rid of you."

"I'm *not* a wench."

He slanted her a look. "Aye, you *are* a wench. You are the reason I got both an unpalatable breakfast and a tongue thrashing from my da the likes of which I haven't suffered since I was a lad. And I doona appreciate it." Stopping abruptly, he backed her up against the wall of the corridor and braced his palms on either side of her head. "So, you and I are going to have an intimate little chat, and you're going to tell me where the hell you came from, and how you came by my plaid. And you will not lie to me, wee English, or you'll regret ever seeking shelter in my castle."

Gwen froze, cradled between his arms. The instinct to touch him, to press her body against him was just as strong as it had been in her time. In fact, it was even stronger, because she'd so recently made love with him. She longed to reach out and brush his unshaven jaw with her fingertips, to caress his hair, to kiss him, to demand that he remember her.

But he was a stranger, and a very angry stranger at that.

"I thought it was Silvan's castle," she said mulishly.

His stare was flat and unamused, with no little silver lights dancing in it. "Then it would have been wiser for you to don Silvan's blue robe, not my plaid. I assure you he is far more accommodating than I. Talk, wench. Whence came you and what is your purpose here?"

"I told your father—"

"I care naught to hear what lies you told my father. 'Twas plain to see how beguiling he found you, but I will not make the same mistake. I doona underestimate you, nor will my wits be disarmed by flouncing hips."

"*Flouncing* hips? I don't flounce," she sputtered. "I have *never* flounced."

"Where are you from?" he repeated icily, crowding her with his big body.

She braced her hands against his chest to hold him at bay. She didn't miss how his eyes flared the moment she touched him.

He knocked them away, and placed his hands back on the wall to either side. "Doona touch me, wench. You know not what you provoke. If I'm going to stand accused of something, I should be able to say I enjoyed it, so doona push me."

Gwen closed her eyes. If he bent much nearer, his lips would be a breath away from hers and she wasn't certain she could prevent herself from wrapping her arms around his neck, pulling him down, and kissing him.

"Open your eyes," he insisted.

Gritting her jaw, she opened her eyes. He was no less domineering in his time than he'd been in hers. "I don't know where I'm from," she said defiantly. "I don't know how I got here. I already told your father that."

He clamped her head in his hands and forced her to meet his gaze. "Tell me that again. Look straight into my eyes and tell me that again."

Gwen drew a deep breath and looked directly into his eyes. *"I don't know how I got here."* That much was certainly true. She had no idea how he'd done what he'd done with the stones.

"Liar. You know me. How do you know me?"

"Do you know me?" she countered cautiously.

"Nay, despite your efforts to make it look as if I took your maidenhead." He paused then added vehemently, "I am not marrying you."

"I didn't *ask* you to."

"Then why did you come here? Why do you act as if you know me?"

Gwen puffed her bangs from her eyes with a soft breath. "Are you certain you don't know me?" she asked tentatively. "You see, I have amnesia," she tried out the lie, "and I don't know if you know me or not."

His silver eyes narrowed and darted from left to right as he scanned her features. It was obvious that she disturbed him on some level. She could sense that he felt a connection that logic insisted couldn't exist. Suddenly she felt almost sorry for him. Almost. If she understood the theories about space-time, technically, he had the memory of her in him somewhere. There had never actually been two different Drustans: only two different fourth- or fifth-dimensional projections of a single set of cells and DNA. Rather like a single ray of light, beamed into a prism and exiting on the other side at multiple angles; one ray of light, just the same. She could imagine how hard a person might work to suppress memories they believed they hadn't lived. Would such memories be perceived as dreams? she wondered. Blurry and vague and nagging?

"I *know* I doona know you. I would recall a woman such as yourself." He paused. "Yet . . ."

"Yet what?" she encouraged, daring to hope. Might he be strong enough of mind to tolerate the memory of two different realities? She could see something in his eyes, she also saw the moment he pushed it away. His scowl faded, and his eyes took on a seductive gleam.

"Yet you look at me with those hungry eyes, like you know me. Or would like to know me." He lowered his head another inch. "Is that what you wish of me, English? To know me?" he purred. "Your maidenhead is gone. Are you so eager to repeat the experience you had last eve?"

She swallowed, mesmerized by him, by the heat in her body, by the lust in his gaze.

Bending near, he brushed his lips against her ear. "There is a mating heat on your skin, and it sets my blood to fire. Shall I ease your discomfort?"

Gwen shivered. *God, she wanted him.*

"I wouldn't care it to be said of me that I left a woman in distress," he said, brushing his lips against her neck. "'Twould ruin my good name."

"Aren't you afraid your father would make you marry me?" she provoked, irritated that he refused to marry her, despite the fact that she wasn't even asking.

"Nay. There are ways around that. And I assure you, 'tis only a matter of time before I discover where you're from. Besides, if you doona recall what happened to you, perhaps you were wed yesterday. Perhaps you already *are* married," he pointed out. "That would certainly explain why you were no longer maiden."

"Then you shouldn't be messing around with someone else's wife," she snapped.

He laughed. "As a rule, I wouldn't. But as I said before, if I'm going to get blamed for the crime, at least I should get the pleasure of committing it. Besides you *want* me. I can feel it. Here," he said, cupping her breasts with his hands. Her nipples crested instantly. "And I see it in your eyes."

Slowly, inexorably, he lowered his mouth to hers.

Why should she resist? She wanted him, plain and simple. And it was clear that the desire he'd felt for her in the
twenty-first century was in no way diminished in the sixteenth. He'd tried to seduce her the moment he'd seen her in
the twenty-first century, and she was glad that he was doing
it again. She liked knowing that he found her desirable in
any place and time. She would greedily take every minute
with him she could get, consequences be damned.

He brushed his lips across hers then pulled back, his eyes
wide. She nearly laughed, because while she knew to expect
the *sizzle* when they touched, he was experiencing it for the
first time. He stared at her until she wet her lip with the tip of
her tongue, then he kissed her, sucking her tongue into his
mouth. Framing her head with his hands, he plunged his
tongue between her lips with the intensity of a drowning
man.

Heat exploded between them.

Nudging her legs apart with a knee, he tugged her forward so she was astride his thigh. He tugged at her nipples
with his fingers, coaxing them to hard crests through her
gown. He kissed her so deeply that he sucked her whimpers
into his mouth.

He was hard and hot and ready, and she was about to
have sex in the middle of a hallway, and not even care about
the impropriety of it.

Back and forth, up and down he rubbed his muscular
thigh between her legs, pinching her nipples, hammering her
with that double-thrust rhythm of tongue and thigh, and
Gwen whimpered into his mouth.

Frantically, she tore at his plaid, desperate to press her
hands against his skin, but he caught them in his and stretched

her arms above her head, securing her wrists against the wall with one hand, while the other resumed a leisurely exploration of her body.

"Let go of my hands," she complained, against his mouth. "I need to touch you."

"Nay. I cannot speak for my actions should you touch me." He sucked her lower lip into his mouth, and made an animal sound deep in his throat.

"You're the one who offered yourself," she mumbled. "Now cooperate."

"I doona offer *all* of me, English." He dropped his head to draw her nipple deeply into his mouth, gown and all. He nipped at the puckered crests, pushed her breasts up and together, and laved the cleavage with his tongue.

"What do you mean, 'all' of you?" she panted, arching her back to give him the best possible access.

"I'm not fool enough to tup you. Silvan would indeed have the final say if I went that far."

Oooh, she was suddenly furious. "Get off me, you oaf!"

He gave her a lazy, incredibly hot grin. "Hush, wee English. I will not leave you wanting. I told you I'd ease your discomfort with my body. I simply didn't tell you which parts of my body I'd be using to do it."

"I will not play childish games with you."

"You'll play any games I ask of you. I doona understand this thing between us, but I know you need what I offer you. And you cannot resist me any more than I can you. I think you've done some witchery to me."

With his demanding mouth, he silenced any reply she might have made and when his hand slipped beneath her gown and up her thigh to the wetness between them, she decided to temporarily abandon her angry thoughts. She'd be angry afterward, she decided, finding a tidy mental compartment for the things she knew she should be feeling, but refused to feel until he was done feeling her.

Ha, she thought—*and men think women can't compartmentalize sex and emotions.*

It took her less than a minute beneath his expert hand to come in shuddering little spasms against him.

He held her for a moment, until her shudders subsided, then placed a finger beneath her chin and tipped her head back.

They stared in silence while time stretched out. His face was tight with lust and she could feel him, rock hard against her thigh. He looked almost angry.

Finally he said, "Come to my bedroom tonight, English."

"To make love? Or for more of this child's play?" Anger popped its unruly head out of its compartment. Perhaps the difference between men and women was not that they didn't compartmentalize, but that women remembered what they'd boxed up for later, while men—with scientifically documented inferior short-term memory—forgot.

"Nay. I cannot bed you. But I promise I will not leave you wanting. Nor will you leave me wanting tonight."

"Dream on." Gwen gathered the tatters of dignity about her and *flounced* down the hall away from him.

But despite her irritation, she was elated. His attraction to her, his inability to turn away from her even though he knew it put him in peril of being forced to wed by his father, was a promising sign. He desired her, and by God, if it was the only way to get his attention, she was going to *flounce* until she drove him crazy.

Drustan leaned back against the wall, folded his arms over his chest, and watched her retreat. He was painfully hard. He rubbed his jaw then caught the scent of her on his hand and got even harder. He closed his eyes and inhaled deeply.

Christ, how could such a tiny woman—the very one he knew he should stay away from if he wished to convince Silvan he hadn't raped her—have such a monumental impact on him? When he'd returned from the village, having learned nothing useful, opened the door and glimpsed her at the top of the stairs, he'd frozen. His tongue had stuck to the roof of his mouth, so dry it had become, and he'd stared like a lovesick lad.

Her body cried out to his in a language that needed no words.

You doona even know her, his mind argued. *'Tis momentary lust, nothing more.*

He shook his head. He'd never felt lust so strong. He'd had no intention of going anywhere near her, then she'd started pinching that luscious lower lip between her finger and thumb, then he'd started imagining nibbling on that lip, and the next thing he'd known, he'd been stalking her with every intention of getting a taste of what he'd been accused of having had already.

He shook his head, furious with himself.

He should stay as far away from her as possible.

He should never touch her again.

He could scarcely *wait* to touch her again . . .

CHAPTER 13

Dinner that night was a disaster. Full-fledged nicotine withdrawal had kicked in, and she was so irritable between pent-up sexual frustration and withdrawal that she doubted her ability to carry on a civil conversation.

The only thought that kept her going was that she knew the physical craving would be greatly diminished in another twenty-four hours. Psychological craving she could handle. It took only about three days to get over the physical withdrawal, but oh, God, it was proving to be a terrible three days. Earlier, while she'd been pacing the castle trying to walk off her irritation, she'd stumbled into a study in the east wing, and had found a box of unusual cigars.

She had taken one out and rolled it in her palms. Sniffed it. Stuck it in her mouth.

But she hadn't smoked it. The only thing that had prevented her was the realization that if she struggled through the next day and a half, the craving would fade, but if she smoked the stupid cigar, she'd only want another one and never break the vicious cycle.

Besides, who wanted cigar breath when she had no toothbrush?

And now, she sat in the Greathall at one of seven long tables. Over a hundred men had come blustering into the keep for dinner. They sat at six of the tables, and absurdly, the seventh long table held only Gwen, Drustan, Silvan, and a young boy named Tristan, whom Silvan had introduced as his protégé.

Drustan had arrived late, and had kicked out the chair at the farthest end of the table from her in silence.

"Brooding, Drustan?" Silvan asked.

Drustan arched a brow. "It depends on what I'm getting for dinner. If it's more pork pie, I'll not just be brooding. I'll be hiring a new cook."

"You'll do no such thing," Silvan snapped. "And if you hurt Nell's feelings, I'll make certain you regret it."

"Do the two of you always fight?" Gwen asked. She'd gotten the impression that Drustan admired his father, yet they seemed forever at each other's throats.

They both looked suddenly abashed.

"Nay," Drustan said. "'Tis just that he picks at me of late—"

"Oh, I pick at you?" Silvan grunted around a mouthful of soup.

Drustan dropped his spoon and held an imaginary hair thong up in his hand. "Tie your hair back, old man. It annoys me."

"Well it does," Drustan said defensively.

"I like Silvan's hair," Gwen said. And she did. She thought he looked wonderfully like a brilliant philosopher or scientist, and he was quite handsome in his own way.

Drustan snorted. "Careful or she'll charm the trews right off you, da."

"Is that what she did to you?" Silvan asked coolly.

Gwen blushed, and Drustan looked down at the table guiltily.

They were saved by the arrival of a gaggle of maids, bearing platters. As they deposited dishes, Gwen dragged her chair closer to Silvan's.

"Who are all these men?" she asked, waving at the other tables.

"Our men-at-arms," he replied, digging into a basket of fresh, warm bread.

"Do they live in the castle?"

"Nay, the garrison is behind the keep. We have over two hundred and fifty men housed in the garrison, and the village of Tillybrand has just under a thousand more. We are a strong clan, and own four manors beyond Tillybrand. Dageus oversees the far-flung ones."

Gwen winced. It wasn't the first time she'd noticed that Silvan, for all his cleverness, still referred to his other son as if he were alive. People had their own ways of dealing with grief, and she supposed his was outright denial.

"What are you two whispering about down there?" Drustan said irritably.

Silvan cocked his head and scowled. "If you'd like to know, join us," he said, gesturing to a seat near Tristan, who was eating in silence.

When Drustan rose from the chair, Gwen's eyes lingered on him hungrily. She couldn't help it. He was wearing his usual tartan, and no leather armor, just a drape of fabric over one shoulder. Powerful dark arms and a sinful glimpse of his rippling abdomen made her bite of bread stick to the roof of her mouth.

"I can see I'm going to have to," he said, tossing a chunk of bread to the floor. It hit with considerable force, and shattered into crusty pieces. "The food isn't as good down at this end," he said, shooting a dark look at Nell who was walking by.

"Maybe that's because the *man* down at that end isn't as good either," she retorted sharply, before bending to scoop the crumbs out of the rushes.

As she was finishing, Drustan tossed a bone from his plat-

ter of ribs over his shoulder.

Only Gwen seemed to notice her sigh as she bent to pick that up, too.

Her eyes narrowed, and she realized Tristan, Silvan—all the men—were doing the same. Whatever they didn't find palatable got chucked over a shoulder. It was no wonder there were rats in the rushes. Poor Nell, as if she didn't have enough to do cooking for hundreds of hungry men. No wonder there were fifty maids in the castle.

"Why are you throwing food on the floor?" she asked Drustan.

"Bones," he said. "I doona eat the bones. Of pigs," he clarified. "Only those of wee young lasses." He flashed an evil grin.

"Do you think Nell enjoys picking them up?" she asked in a voice that dripped icicles. Behind Drustan's shoulder, Nell paused and glanced at Gwen, obviously interested in this.

"What?" Drustan said, pretending not to understand.

"Nell. The sweet, kind woman who is in her fifties and probably can't bend over with the same agility she had twenty years ago. Nothing against you, Nell," she added as an after-thought. "On that note," she said, rising to her feet as her temper rose, "do you think the maids enjoy having to clean out rat-infested rushes every week? Has it occurred to you that you could do without the rushes entirely if you simply quit throwing things on the floor? And maybe then the maids could scrub these stones down and have a hope of keeping them clean. Perhaps it wouldn't smell like a pigsty in here. Do you think it might not be beyond you to simply lay the pieces you don't want beside your plate?" By the time she'd finished, every maid in the room had stopped serving and was looking at Drustan who looked absolutely bewildered by her assault.

"We've always—"

"I don't care what you've always done. It's rude and inconsiderate."

In the pregnant silence that followed, in which nearly every maid in the room and most of the guards placed mental bets on how long it would take the laird to kill the wee lass, Silvan broke the tension by laughing. His shoulders shook with merriment, and in a few moments, Nell came to stand behind him and joined him.

They laughed and laughed while everyone in the hall stared at them as if they'd gone mad. When finally they stopped laughing and Silvan patted Nell's hand, which had somehow ended upon his shoulder, Drustan said, "You would let her speak to us like that? You will explain yourself, da."

"Nay. I'll do no such thing." Silvan returned to his soup with gusto. "However, I do believe the lass has a point. We *have* been making more work for Nell, and I personally would like to see the end of these damned rushes, perhaps a few rugs on clean stones. The new rule is: If you doona like it, lie it beside your plate. Anyone who tosses food on the floor, sleeps on the floor."

"I already sleep on the floor," Tristan said. Then he looked horrified, as if he'd spoken when he wasn't supposed to.

"He does?" Gwen was appalled.

"On a pallet on the floor, outside my chamber. 'Tis standard for an apprentice." He cut Tristan a look. "Explain to her that you're happy to do it."

"It's all right, milady." Tristan glanced guiltily at Silvan. "To become a Druid, I'd sleep in the snow, if I had to."

A tense silence blanketed the table, and she saw a muscle in Silvan's jaw twitch before he dropped his head so she couldn't see his expression. She glanced at Drustan, whose face had gone pale.

Finally, Silvan raised his head from his soup and said brightly, "He's a fanciful lad, my Tristan. I'm teaching him numbers."

Gwen inclined her head, something inside her going very still. Pretending nothing was amiss, she helped herself to a selection of ribs and roasted potatoes, all the while her mind was churning.

To become a Druid, Tristan had said. *Druids. These men are Druids. Now I'm getting somewhere.*

The rest of the dinner passed in uneventful silence, which was fine with her, because she was tired and needed to get back to her room to make some notes.

First plan on the agenda tomorrow: get that boy Tristan alone.

THE DARK
HIGHLANDER
LITE

It's enough that I know that you're out there somewhere,
buying a used copy of Nietzsche's Beyond Good and Evil
from a street vendor for a quarter.

This one's for you, my most worthy adversary.

Dear Reader,

I call this The Dark Highlander Lite.

My fourth novel, Kiss of the Highlander *was released on September 4, 2001. Precisely one week later, it hit the* New York Times *extended bestseller list. It stayed on the list for three weeks, a rarity for a romance novel in those times. The day it hit the list was 9/11/01, a day so filled with tragedy that it eclipsed any personal joy I might have felt. Instead, I felt guilt that took me a long time to shake. How could one of my books hit the* New York Times *bestseller list the same day New York, and the whole country, suffered such tragic loss? Rationally the two had nothing to do with each other. My heart remained unconvinced and refused to celebrate.*

Shortly after 9/11, I moved from inner city Cincinnati to a quieter place in rural Indiana. In the months following the attack, I struggled to re-acclimate to the world I'd thought I knew. I had a book due and wasn't remotely in the mood to start writing, but meeting my deadlines pays my bills, so I sat down to write when the last thing I wanted was danger and adventure. I wanted comfort.

During November, December, and part of January I wrote two hundred and fifty pages of The Dark Highlander, *version one. Sometime in February, I took a hard look at it and was stunned at how wrong it had come out. It wasn't the version I'd intended to write at all. I'd written a clone of Drustan because Drustan was comforting to me. Dageus isn't comforting. He's dark, tortured, and intensely sexual. Though twins, the brothers are night and day. Drustan is noble, honorable, and would never* tell a lie. Dageus would break any rule for love. Drustan is comfort. Dageus is excitement. Drustan makes love. Dageus fucks. I wanted my reader to put The Dark Highlander down when they were done and think "Wow, there were three main characters in that book: Dageus, Chloe, and Sex." Version one was so far off track I was astounded, as if I'd been writing in a daze, which I was. A lot of us wandered in various degrees of disconnect for months after 9/11.

There I sat with nearly two-thirds of a book that was due in a month, and it was the wrong book. I called my editor and told her I was throwing it away and starting over. After she finished completely freaking out, she asked me to send it in anyway, let her take a look at it and decide. I refused because I was afraid if I sent it in she would try to publish it, and there was no way I was going to let that happen. She promised me they wouldn't unless they thought it was good enough and I told her that was the problem: It was good enough.

It wasn't the right story.

It was easier before I became a fairly decent writer to decide what to throw away and what to keep. Once your writing achieves a certain level of competence, it can be tricky to discern if it also has the right stuff. Version one was more than competent; it was fun and entertaining but it didn't have the darkness or the magic that I could see in my head, yet had failed to translate to the page.

It was a terrifying moment for me. I'd never missed a deadline. I didn't have time to miss a deadline because I get paid when I turn the book in and I needed the money. Delaying it six months meant hard financial times and a great deal of uncertainty. Still, the book wasn't what I wanted for Dageus. It wasn't true to the vision I'd had when I first decided to tell *the story of my Keltar brothers. I remember feeling poised on a precipice. If I jumped off into the land of "okay, I let the wrong version get published and I'll live with it," I might never be able to stand on the edge of that precipice and hold my ground. It was a defining moment. I've never regretted the choice I made. You have to draw your lines in the sand and stay them.*

We agreed that I would take a week, start the "right" version, and I would send her fifty pages of each. What she didn't know was that I burned all but fifty pages of version one so I wouldn't be tempted.

After she read them both, she extended my deadline, and I started over. She said if she'd never read the first fifty pages of version two she might have thought I was crazy, but once she read it, she saw exactly what I meant. The Dark Highlander Lite *was good. But* The Dark Highlander *Dark rocked* it.

I thought version one was gone forever but recently my computer guys restored a few dead hard drives and old Zip discs and guess what I'd backed up? Here's the first part of The Dark Highlander Lite *that was never published. It's a rough draft, unedited. That means no line or conceptual editing, so you've been warned.*

It's fun stuff, warm and sexy, with glimpses into the world of the Keltar you won't find anywhere else. And it was the wrong story. Email me at karen@karenmoning.com after you read it and let me know what you think.

Unfortunately there can be no doubt that man is, on the whole, less good than he imagines himself or wants to be. Everyone carries a Shadow . . .

—Carl Jung

'Tis no' the way of Evil to assault. True Evil seduces.

—*Book of Midhe*

PROLOGUE

THOUSANDS OF YEARS BEFORE THE BIRTH OF CHRIST, THERE settled in Ireland a race called the Tuatha Dé Danann who, over time, became known as the True Race or the Fairy.

An advanced civilization from a faraway place, the Tuatha Dé Danann educated in Druid ways some of the more promising humans they encountered. For a time, man and "fairy" shared the earth in peace, but sadly, bitter dissension arose between them, and the Tuatha Dé Danann decided to move on. Legend claims they were driven "under the hills" into "fairy mounds." The truth is they never left our world, but hold their fantastic court in places difficult for humans to find.

After the Tuatha Dé Danann left, the human Druids warred among themselves for power. Thirteen of their once-faithful Druids turned to dark ways and—thanks to what the Tuatha Dé Danann had taught them—nearly destroyed the earth.

Incensed, the Tuatha Dé Danann emerged from their hidden

places and stopped the Druids moments before they succeeded in damaging the earth beyond repair. They punished the Druids who'd turned evil by casting them into a place between dimensions, locking their immortal souls in an eternal prison.

The Tuatha Dé Danann then selected a noble bloodline, the Keltar, to use the sacred knowledge to rebuild and nurture the land. Together, they negotiated The Compact: the treaty governing cohabitation of their races. The Keltar swore many oaths to the Tuatha Dé Danann, first and foremost that they would never use the power of the standing stones—which give the man who knows the sacred formulas the ability to move through space and time—for personal motives or political ends. The Tuatha Dé Danann pledged many things in return, first and foremost that they would never spill the lifeblood of a mortal. Both races have long abided by the pledges made that day.

Over the ensuing millennia, the MacKeltar journeyed to Scotland and settled in the Highlands above what is now called Inverness. Although most of their ancient history from the time of their involvement with the Tuatha Dé Danann has melted into the mists of their distant past and been forgotten, and although the Keltar clan has not encountered a Tuathan in over two thousand years (giving rise to speculation that the ancient race no longer exists), they have never strayed from their sworn purpose.

The MacKeltar pledged to serve the greater good of the world. On the few occasions they have opened a gate to other times within the circle of stones, it has been for the noblest of reasons: to protect the earth from great peril. An ancient legend holds that if a MacKeltar breaks his oath and uses the stones to travel through time for personal motive, the myriad souls of the darkest Druids trapped in the in-between will claim him and make him the most evil, terrifyingly powerful Druid humankind has ever known.

In the fifteenth century, twin brothers Drustan and Dageus MacKeltar are born. As their ancestors before them, they protect the ancient lore, nurture the land, and guard the coveted secret of the standing stones. Honorable men, without corruption, Dageus and Drustan serve faithfully.

Until one fateful night, in a moment of blinding grief, Dageus MacKeltar violates the sacred Compact.

When his brother, Drustan, is killed, Dageus enters the circle of stones and goes back in time to prevent Drustan's death. He succeeds, but between dimensions, he is taken by the souls of the evil Druids, who have not tasted or touched or smelled anyone or anything, nor made love nor danced nor vied for power, for nearly four thousand years.

Hungry, determined to live again, they urge him to use his immense power for their corrupt purposes. The Druids wish him to go back in time to change the outcome of their fateful battle thousands of years' past—and utterly re-create history as we've known it.

Now Dageus MacKeltar is a man with one good conscience— and thirteen bad ones. Although he can hold his own for a while, his time is growing short.

1

D RUSTAN MACKELTAR FINISHED READING THE LETTER
from his da, Silvan, and cursed bitterly.

When he crushed the fragile parchment in his hand, the
centuries-old fabric disintegrated in his fist. 'Twas no matter,
he thought grimly, for the words were forever carved into his
mind as if scored there by a hissing red-hot blade.

Drustan, my son, I have missed you, it had begun so inno-
cently, to end so badly—

> *I wish you might have met your brothers and sisters, but
> your heart was with Gwen, and 'twas where it wisely be-
> longed. I wish the two of you every happiness, but rue to tell
> you your trials are not yet o'er.*
>
> *First, the gentler news. Beloved Nell consented to be my
> wife. She has made every moment a joy. We left a few
> things for the two of you in the tower. Count over three*

stones on the base of the slab, second stone from the bottom. Life has been rich and full, more than I e'er dreamed. I have no regrets, but one.

I should have watched Dageus more closely after you went into the tower. I should have seen what was happening. There you slumbered, enchanted, waiting to awaken in the twenty-first century and be reunited with Gwen, while here I sat, cozy with my Nell.

Yet Dageus grew e'er more solitary. Blinded by my own happiness, I didn't see what was happening until it was too late. I shall be scant with the details, but suffice it to say as time passed, he became . . . obsessed with you. He worried that something would happen to prevent you from surviving until you found Gwen again.

And it did. I have no memory of it, mayhap an odd wrinkle in my mind, but he confessed to me that three years after we placed your enchanted body in the northeast tower, that wing of the castle caught fire and you were burned and died.

Dageus broke his oath, went back in time through the stones to the day of the fire, and prevented the fire from occurring. He saved you, but in so doing, turned Dark. The old legends were true.

If you are reading this, he succeeded in his course, for he appointed himself your dark guardian; his sole purpose to see you awaken safely at the proper time in the future. He vowed to watch over you, then disappeared. Dageus is a strong man, and I believe such a vow has kept him sane. I hope it has, for I tasted the evil within him.

I believe, however, the moment you awaken and are reunited with your wife, there will be nothing to hold his

darkness at bay. His purpose accomplished, the thin thread
that binds him to the light will snap.

Och, my son, 'tis sorry I am to be sayin' this, but you
must find him. You must save him. And if you cannot save
him, you must kill him.

Nay! Drustan longed to roar. *Nay and nay—it cannot be so!*
His reunion with his beloved wife had been purchased at
no less than the cost of his brother's very soul.

He stared blindly at the portraits Christopher had un-
veiled scant minutes past: portraits Dageus himself had
painted back in the sixteenth century, so they might be passed
down from generation to generation, a warning to all future
Keltars.

A warning to Drustan. *I am dark. You must find a way to*
destroy me, read the Pict runes carved into the frames of the
portraits.

Damn you, Dageus, he raged silently. *Damn you—you*
should have let me die.

"Oh, Drustan!" Gwen's voice broke as she rushed to his
side and took his hands in hers. The remnants of the parchment dusted the floor when she twined her fingers with his.
He held on to her. Tight.

She'd been silent while he'd read the letter aloud, translat-
ing the bitter message into English. His distant descendant,
Christopher, who'd given him the cursed letter from his da,
had also been silent, standing near the fire with his wife,
Maggie.

Gwen's silence he understood, because she'd been stunned
and horrified. But Christopher, who spoke *Gàidhlig,* had
known exactly what the letter said. Indeed, had known since

long before Drustan had awakened in the twenty-first century, a fortnight past.

Thus wasting an entire fortnight that Drustan might have put to good use, searching for Dageus.

"Why didn't you tell me sooner?" Drustan thundered.

Christopher blew out a pent breath. "Because you'd only just awakened and we thought—"

"You thought *wrong*!"

"—to find him for you," the tall, muscular Scot finished. "And we have," he added evenly. "He's no' exactly kept a low profile. Sixteenth-century coins in mint condition and a few Keltar blades recently appeared on the antiquities market. It was an easy matter to trace the address of the seller. He's rented rooms under his own name. It's my belief he *wants* you to find him."

"Where is he?" Drustan roared.

"In Edinburgh," Maggie replied softly. "And there's no need to shout and get angry with my husband. It was my doing as well. We saw no sense in telling you 'til we had some idea where he might be found. Or even *when* he might be found. From the paintings and Silvan's letter, we suspected he might come to this century, if only to make sure you awakened safely. That he remains here is promising. We located him but a few days ago. Christopher passed the day in Edinburgh yesterday, watching him from a distance. Thus far, he's evidenced no signs of . . . overt . . ." Maggie trailed off uncomfortably.

"Evil?" Drustan said, his voice suddenly deceptively soft. His gaze snapped back to Christopher. "You were watching my brother and didn't tell me?" A muscle in his jaw worked as he clamped his teeth together in an effort not to shout.

"I'm a Keltar, too, Drustan," Christopher reminded. "We're both responsible for him."

"We'll save him, Drustan," Gwen said softly, slipping her arms around his waist. "There are four of us MacKeltars, and we're a formidable lot. We'll bring him home and we'll help him. Dageus is *not* evil. I refuse to believe that."

Drustan gazed down at the woman he loved more than life itself, relaxing, if only minutely. She always had that effect on him; made the world seem a better place, full of hope and possibility and dreams. His arms tightened around her. *So, she is my gift from you, eh, brother?* he thought darkly. *My lovely, brilliant wife that I'd ne'er have seen again, if not for your sacrifice. Damn you, brother.*

Then another thought, accompanied by waves of suffocating guilt: *Thank you, brother.*

Tears shimmered on his wife's cheeks and Drustan nearly envied her the release of weeping.

But there would be no tears shed by Drustan MacKeltar because tears meant grieving and grieving meant ruing the losing, and he would have naught to rue because he would not be losing his brother.

Not even if it meant he had to do battle with the ancient Druids himself to win back Dageus's soul.

You must save him, Silvan's letter had said.

And as far as Drustan was concerned, Silvan's letter had ended there.

2

NOVEMBER 27TH, HARVARD UNIVERSITY

"A PACKAGE JUST ARRIVED FOR YOU, MS. ZANDERS," DR. BEN-pohl barked as they passed each other in the hallway. "A rather large package." He peered irritably at her down his long thin nose. His nostrils were white around the edges; a sure sign he was in a temper. "It's blocking my view out the window. See that you take care of it promptly. You know how I feel about clutter. It's bad enough that we have to share an office. The least you can do is respect that it's my space, too. *You* may enjoy living in the midst of chaos. *I* don't."

"And good morning to you, too," Elisabeth muttered, scowling at his tall, lanky frame as he marched down the hallway.

Monday mornings were bad enough. Coffee made them better. Grumpy men made them worse. And one thing she could always count on was Dr. Richard Benpohl being grumpy. Something so simple as a smile from the man might make her think she'd lost her mind. Not that he didn't smile, he simply never smiled at *her,* and he never would.

A card-carrying member of the Old Boy's School, Dr. Benpohl refused to believe that a mere woman, regardless of her impressive IQ, and excellent scholastic record, could possibly contribute a thing to Harvard's Human Development and Psychology Department.

So she and the "Beanpole," as she called him in the privacy of her mind, spent most of their time sharing an office, glaring at each other over their work—he at his spotless desk graced by only a laptop, a brass lamp, and a nameplate; she perched amid haphazard piles of books and articles that she just *knew* she might get to one day—marveling that the other managed so simple a task as putting their shoes on the right feet in the morning.

In her more honest moments, she admitted that they both suffered from a bit of prejudice, for Elisabeth had little respect for a male's ability to delve into the human psyche. Most men she knew didn't have the faintest clue why they behaved the way they did, and if they lacked a reason, they dredged up the timeless excuse of testosterone. *I didn't* mean *to sleep with her but she had breasts.*

Men!

Wrinkling her nose, Elisabeth entered their shared office at a brisk pace. She'd give anything to meet a man capable of honest introspection. A man who had a bit of darkness in him, for she agreed with Carl Jung that only a man who knew his own shadow was capable of deep, abiding love. She wanted a man who believed in things like fidelity, commitment, and happily-ever-after. A man who *meant* forever when he said forever, unlike most men she knew. And, while she was at it, she thought—snorting at herself for such silly, impossible wishing—*handsome, passionate, an undying romantic, and hung like a*—

She drew up short, her wistful thoughts dashed, startled by the package that had so offended the Beanpole.

It was rather obtrusive, she admitted grudgingly. A foot taller than her, and four or five feet wide, the heavy wooden crate was indeed blocking the entire window, and most of the east wall. Sighing, she smoothed her hair, absently making sure every curly strand was snugly tucked in her plait, then busied herself at the microwave, peeking curiously at the crate as she nuked a cup of water and stirred in three heaping teaspoons of instant coffee. *The hell with it,* she thought, adding a fourth—*oh, blessed caffeine*—she had a feeling she was going to need it this morning.

Nudging books aside so she might lean back against a corner of her desk without causing an avalanche, she was momentarily distracted by Benpohl's most recent invasion of her privacy.

He'd poked through the organized chaos on her desk and dug out several romance novels that she'd picked up at the used bookstore yesterday on her lunch break but had forgotten to take home last night. He'd stacked them smack in the center, and with the instincts of a shark had placed on top one with a particularly revealing cover, showcasing a mostly nude man, handcuffed, awaiting a lovely blond woman with the key. He'd stuck a Post-it on it that read: ARE WE HAVING ID PROBLEMS, MS. ZANDERS? TRASH. ABSOLUTE TRASH.

"At least I only fantasize about it and don't act on it," she muttered.

The only reason you don't act on it, her id seethed, *is because you work so much that you don't have time for a life. Get out and play. Take a vacation. Get laid, Zanders.*

"Quit needling me. And watch your language," she said irritably. She only had one more year until she was finished with her Ph.D. She had every intention of getting a life then. Maybe. If it didn't conflict with her career ambitions.

Life now! her id insisted. *We could die tomorrow.*

Sighing, she refused to get sucked into the age-old argument. The id was the pleasure seeker, interested only in instant gratification. Were her id in control of things, she'd be walking around with a mattress strapped to her back.

Snatching up the romance novel, she stuffed it in a drawer, shoved the rest beneath her desk, then perched on the cluttered edge of it and eyed the crate while sipping her coffee.

Whatever was in the crate was going to have to wait until her classes were finished for the day, because she was already running late. As she scooped up her notes, she took a last quick glance at the package, wondering what might be in it and who it was from. Based on the shape of the crate, and its shallow depth, it looked like it might be a painting, but she certainly hadn't purchased a painting recently, or anything for that matter. Not on the pathetic living allowance that came with her fellowship.

Scotland, she mused, as her gaze fell on the postmark. She left the office and closed the door. The darn thing had been shipped from Scotland. Go figure . . .

———

When Gwen entered the study, Drustan glanced up from the aged scroll he was studying.

"Having any luck?" Gwen asked softly, knowing what

the answer was going to be from the despair etched in every line of her husband's face.

Drustan shook his head, his silvery eyes dark. "And it doesn't help that we're missing some of the oldest tomes. Christopher said they were destroyed in the late seventeenth century when a MacKeltar took a wife who grew to fear her husband's 'pagan' ways and tried to put an end to his dabbling in the dark arts by setting a fire in the tower library. We can't find the *Book of Midhe,* nor any of the *Books of Manannán,* not to mention dozens of others." He laid the scroll aside and rose from behind the mound of books and parchments on his desk. "How fare you? Have you heard from the lass you sent the portrait to?"

"I just shipped it last week," Gwen replied, skirting the piles of books that were scattered across the floor, and spilling from ottomans and curio tables. She snuggled into her husband's embrace. When his hands slipped to her heavily rounded abdomen, she smiled. Even six months into her pregnancy, Drustan still sought daily reassurance that it was true; that they would soon be welcoming twins into the world. "She should receive it any day now," she continued, as she tipped her head back, and studied him with loving concern. His eyes were tired and red-rimmed from poring over books and parchments. It was all she could do to get him to wolf down the occasional sandwich or cup of coffee. For the past three and a half months he and Christopher had been scouring the old lore, laboring over ancient translations, up to eighteen hours a day.

They had yet to discover a single passage about those they'd taken to calling "the thirteen." She grazed her hands lightly over his face as if she might brush his weariness away. He turned his face into her hands and kissed her palms.

"Are you certain bringing her here is wise, Gwen?" he asked wearily.

"With Elisabeth's training in psychology she may be able to think of something we can't, Drustan. Something to help him hold the druids at bay until we find the way to cure him." She suppressed a flash of guilt for concealing her deeper motives, but she suspected that if Drustan knew what she was up to, he'd put a stop to it. He'd argue it was too dangerous.

"You truly believe this lass will just drop everything and come rushing o'er to Scotland?"

Gwen smiled. "If I know Elisabeth half as well as I think I do, once she sees the portrait we sent her, she won't be able to resist."

Elisabeth had completely forgotten about the package by the time she finally returned to her office that evening.

The Beanpole had not forgotten. He'd plastered it with dozens of Post-its for the janitorial service that said: TRASH. PLEASE REMOVE IMMEDIATELY.

Gritting her teeth, Elisabeth plucked the offensive Post-its from the package, balled them up, and tossed them in random disarray on the Beanpole's neat-as-a-pin desk. It was hell sharing an office with someone she didn't like. Just walking in the door some mornings raised her blood pressure twenty points.

Dropping her notes on a chair, she eyed the crate. Her curiosity piqued, she rummaged through the Beanpole's desk for a screwdriver, happily mussing everything and—feeling childish but unable to resist—depositing one wet and thoroughly chewed piece of gum atop a tidy pad of Post-its in his top drawer, then went to work prying the crate open.

A painting indeed, she thought a few minutes later as she awkwardly hefted the large, heavily wrapped item from the crate. There was a thick, creamy envelope taped to the wrapping, with her name scrawled on it in handwriting that was vaguely familiar.

She considered the letter and the package a moment, then chose the package. Propping it up against the crate, she began peeling away the brown paper wrapping.

The first strip she tore off revealed a man's nipple.

Now that's more like it, her id purred and, for a change, Elisabeth echoed the sentiment. She might not give men much credit for emotional maturity, and she might prefer to keep them safely at arm's length so they couldn't get close only to go walking out at a critical moment, but she certainly could appreciate eye candy.

The second strip she pulled away revealed a man's navel, centered in rippling muscle.

"Wow," she breathed, as she fell to unwrapping it with enthusiasm. *Wouldn't the Beanpole just have a freaking heart attack if he walked in now?* she thought, laughing softly.

She bared more of it in strips. A grassy knoll. A night sky. A brilliant purple-and-black tartan, that ended above powerfully muscled calves and clung to lean hips. More of that sculpted stomach and chest. Strong arms and broad, powerful shoulders. All the makings of a woman's most primitive fantasy . . .

The laughter died abruptly in her throat as she tore off the last remaining strip, revealing the magnificent man's face.

Er . . . faces, she amended uneasily. For the man had *two,* and the breath hitched in her throat.

She stared in silence for a long, long time, feeling something stir within her that made her deeply uneasy. Curiosity. Fascination. An intense unbidden flash of sensual awareness.

For heaven's sake, she chided herself, blowing out an uneasy breath, *it's only a picture!*

But it was more than that. He radiated a barely harnessed, fantastic energy. The man—and he was every inch raw male, dripping dark, intoxicating sexuality—had been painted standing on a grassy slope, with silhouettes of standing stones behind him. The night sky was the backdrop; a velvety canvas pierced by glittering stars. Clad in only a kilt, he was magnificent, with skin like golden velvet poured over steel, a sculpted physique, and silky, black-as-midnight hair that spilled down his back and over one shoulder. His chiseled face was exotic, almost impossibly beautiful.

But the beauty ended abruptly, or rather, to the *left* it ended, for the man's face turned both ways. One face turned right, breathtakingly handsome, with glittering golden eyes, firm pink lips, an arrogant blade of a nose, and a strong jaw. Stunningly male, stunningly sensual, it made places low in her belly feel tight.

The other face turned to the left was evil incarnate. The eyes were completely black, with no whites. The sensual lips were pulled back in an animalistic snarl. Whereas the face to the right dripped heat and a playful sexuality, the face turned to the left was hard, aloof, and icy. Powerful. Dangerous.

Dark as sin. And intensely seductive. In a dangerous kind of a-smart-girl-would-run-like-hell way.

What kind of painting was this? And why had it been sent to *her*?

Feeling strangely breathless, Elisabeth fumbled for the envelope and tore it open. Withdrawing a thick sheet of expensive linen paper, she tossed the envelope on her desk, unfolded the letter, and glanced first at the signature.

Gwen Cassidy, she thought, smiling at the memory of her brilliant physicist friend with the warped sense of humor. Although they'd known each other for only two semesters, they'd bonded instantly, sharing complaints about the bureaucratic political nightmare that Harvard could often be, a common and general distrust of men, a mutual loathing of "short jokes," and a love of romance novels, the steamier the better.

They'd met when Elisabeth had been in her second year of undergrad, and Gwen in her second year of the Ph.D. program. One of the most promising up-and-coming theoretical physicists Harvard had ever boasted, Gwen had suddenly dropped out midterm and disappeared. Shortly thereafter, she'd sent Elisabeth a brief note, with no return address, apologizing and promising to be in touch soon. A promise she'd not kept.

Elisabeth had missed her and had often wondered what had become of her. Why was she writing to her now? And what was the deal with the painting?

Merely thinking of it drew her gaze, and it had the same impact on her again. Her breath caught in her throat and she got a funny feeling in her stomach. Poor man, she thought. So tortured, so . . . lost.

So incredibly sexy.

She forced her gaze back to the letter.

Dear Elisabeth, it began, *I know it's been a long time. I hope you remember me! I'm married now, and the man in the portrait is my husband's brother. Enclosed is a check for ten thousand dollars.*

Ten thousand dollars! Elisabeth snatched the envelope off the desk, and sure enough, there it was, tucked inside. Payable to Elisabeth Zanders. Ten thousand lovely dollars. She gaped at the check for a moment, decided that kissing it would be tacky, then returned her attention to the letter.

Please purchase your plane tickets and whatever else you may need for a stay in Scotland. Your salary will be fifty thousand dollars—

"What?" Elisabeth gasped.

—for three months of your time. (Did I mention my husband is rich?) If you're able to help Dageus, you'll receive a bonus of double that. When might we expect you? Oh, and by the way, it's a self-portrait. Dageus painted it of himself.

The letter dropped from Elisabeth's suddenly nerveless fingers. Eyeing it warily, she peered down at it. Then she knelt beside it.

It *did* say fifty thousand dollars.

Elisabeth snatched up the letter.

Call me. Followed by a phone number.

"But I'm not qualified, Gwen," Elisabeth shakily informed the empty office. She remained on her knees because they felt too wobbly to hold her at the moment. Fifty thousand dollars would change her life. Teetering perpetually on the brink of financial disaster, she lived in a spartan efficiency apartment, and had been surviving on Bumble Bee tuna and mac and cheese for far too long. While her fellowship covered her tuition, the meager stipend she got for living expenses barely kept her head above water. "I'm just a student. I've never done any real counseling. I haven't even finished my Ph.D. yet." Not to mention that she still had her internship, dissertation, and up to two years of supervised practice to complete before she could get licensed.

I know you don't have your degree yet, and I know you aren't licensed, but that's okay. I recently corresponded with Dr. Taylor and he told me that you're the finest in the department. (He couldn't say enough good things about you!) I think you're perfect for the job.

"What job? What exactly is wrong with him?" Elisabeth wondered aloud.

"And now you're bringing pornography into our office," observed a dry, disgusted voice behind her. "As if those trashy novels aren't bad enough."

"Dr. Benpohl!" Elisabeth jumped up, clutching both letter and check tightly to her chest.

"I suppose you're going to tell me that since he has two faces, it's somehow work related? Split personalities and all, *hmm?* I know I should be more tolerant, but Ms. Zanders, I really wish you'd get the hell out of this office. And my life. For good."

Elisabeth eyed Dr. Benpohl a long moment. Then she glanced back at the portrait. Then back at Dr. Benpohl. Then at the largest check she'd ever held in her hands. Made payable to *her.*

Live now, her id urged.

It has nothing to do with living, she rebuked silently, *this is a career decision.* Being hired to work with a patient before she'd even completed her degree would enhance her already impressive credentials, and provide fodder for her impending dissertation.

A personal sabbatical wouldn't be too difficult to arrange. Although Benpohl didn't like her, he was the only person in the department who didn't. She could file for a leave, and be on her way in a week, maybe less. The job would get her away from the Beanpole, and that in itself was an irresistible temptation.

And the money—fifty thousand dollars and a possible bonus! It seemed too good to be true!

But that man . . .

Elisabeth glanced back at the painting, firmly suppressing a flash of unease. Surely he didn't really look like that in real life. No man was that attractive. He'd probably, suffering delusions of grandeur, painted himself twenty times more attractive than he actually was. Not to mention that he'd painted himself wearing a kilt, she mused, as if he fancied himself a medieval warrior or something equally silly. *I bet he's a foot or two shorter, balding, and overweight,* she consoled herself with the thought.

She wondered what his problem might be. It couldn't be multiple personalities as the Beanpole had proposed, because treatment for that kind of condition took years of expert therapy. Whatever his problem was, she mused, fifty thousand dollars was definitely incentive to try. Were Grandma Maggie still alive, even she, who'd taught her to always err on the side of caution, would have agreed.

She was going to do it, she realized with a thrill. When

was the last time she'd done something so spur of the moment?

Uh . . . can you say never? her id commented dryly. *And you'd better burn a bridge behind you so you can't change your mind.*

Suddenly feeling as if a huge weight had been lifted from her shoulders, feeling giddy in fact, Elisabeth could think of one bridge she'd relish torching. Drawing a deep breath, she flashed her nemesis the first and only genuine smile he would ever receive from her. A farewell-and-good-riddance smile. A you-are-a-bug-beneath-my-shoe-and-these-shoes-are-walking smile. The thought of not having to see him every morning was intoxicating. "You know what, Beanpole—"

"*Benpohl,*" he snapped.

"I'm going to do just that. Leave, that is. You can take this office and stuff . . ."

The rest of what she said she'd never repeat in polite company, but there were times when getting things off one's chest was positively cathartic. Repression bad, heartfelt communication good.

Psychology could be *so* simple.

———

"Did you tell her anything about his, er . . . condition?" Drustan asked.

"How could I?" Gwen said, with a little sigh. "Write her a letter and tell her that I married a sixteenth-century Highland laird whose brother is possessed—"

"I despise that word, Gwen," Drustan said softly.

"Whose brother is sharing cranial space with thirteen ancient Druids," she corrected.

"It does come off rather badly either way, doesn't it?" Drustan said, wincing.

"She'd never believe it. In fact, she'd come rushing over here to treat *me*. I'm counting on the advance and the painting to get her here. Once she's here, I'm counting on the salary I promised to keep her here."

"But when she arrives, what then?"

"I'm not sure, Drustan," Gwen said. Tucking her fringed bangs behind her ear, she sighed pensively. "I guess I'm hoping the details will sort themselves out along the way. All I know is that it could take you and Christopher *years* to translate all the books and documents up in Silvan's old tower, and Dageus doesn't have years. He may not have months. I can't sit around, watching him get worse, and do nothing. If there's any chance at all that she can help him, we have to try." Her eyes misted with tears. Watching Dageus suffer, watching her husband frantically searching for a way to save him, was breaking her heart.

Drustan's gaze softened. He kissed her, murmuring encouragement that she do what she thought best. Which made her feel doubly guilty for not telling him precisely how she hoped the details might sort themselves.

It wasn't exactly Elisabeth's professional expertise she was after.

No psychologist was going to be able to solve Dageus's problem; it simply wasn't that kind of problem. Dageus being lonely and not having a mate of his own was part of what had gotten him into this mess to begin with. After much consideration, she'd concluded that the only thing that might be able to save him was the power of love.

A woman's love.

Something worth fighting for.

Granted, it was a gamble, but there wasn't much left to lose.

While Drustan and Christopher concentrated their efforts on an exhaustive search through the hundreds of Keltar journals and records and books—a search she feared would yield nothing—Gwen intended to pin her hopes on a good old-fashioned miracle. Funny, she mused, a year ago she hadn't believed in anything that couldn't be explained by science, and now here she was angling for divine intervention. Heavens, how meeting her husband and falling so deeply in love had changed her!

"Trust me, Drustan," Gwen said softly. "I think Elisabeth Zanders might be just what Dageus needs."

And, with the mysterious logic of a pregnant woman who'd found love where she'd least expected it—at the bottom of a treacherous ravine at that—she suspected that Dageus MacKeltar might just be what Elisabeth needed, too.

3

INVERNESS, SCOTLAND, TEN DAYS LATER

B Y THE TIME ELISABETH ARRIVED IN INVERNESS, SHE WAS no longer feeling giddy. In fact, she was exhausted and seriously questioning her sanity for dropping everything and rushing off to Scotland.

Resting her head on the steering wheel of the recently wrecked rental car, she tried to summon the energy to climb out and announce herself at the MacKeltar's castle.

And just where is Gwen, anyway? she wondered wearily, rubbing her eyes.

She'd been up since five o'clock yesterday morning. She'd forced herself to get up early so that when she caught the ten p.m. flight out of Boston that night, she'd sleep through most of the flight. She'd planned to wake up bright and cheery in London, gracefully adjust to the five-hour time difference, and spend her six-hour layover happily devouring the latest Nora Roberts novel.

As if.

On the flight over she'd been wedged into a seat between two young boys whose parents had cleverly requested seats ten rows behind them and had been blissfully snoring away before the plane had even taken off. The boys, positively bristling with excitement, had pestered Elisabeth with nonstop questions. When she'd finally closed her eyes and pretended to sleep, the boys had whipped out Game Boys and for the duration of the flight her eardrums had been assaulted by a metallic *bleep-bleep-ZOOP!* What fitful sleep she'd managed to snatch had been full of creepy little monsters stalking her with ray guns.

Upon landing in London, she'd tried to make up the lost sleep on a bench in an out-of-the-way corner, but had belatedly discovered that the coffee in the airport apparently had some kind of illegal stimulant in it. For the entire six hours, she'd sat bug-eyed and jittery, worrying about whether she'd turned the iron off before she'd left, set the thermostat high enough that the pipes wouldn't freeze, and myriad other nagging details.

By the time she'd arrived at Inverness airport at five-thirty Scotland time, she'd been awake for thirty-one hours straight and was having a hard time concentrating on simple tasks like making sure her zipper was up after going to the restroom. She'd loitered in a sleep-deprived fog at the airport for another two hours, waiting for Gwen to pick her up, before it finally occurred to her to call and find out what was keeping her.

No one answered at the number she'd been given.

Never one to admit defeat, she'd trudged off to rent a car, only to find the steering wheel on the right side, which was unequivocally—to anyone in their right mind—the wrong side of the car. Oh, she'd known Europeans drove funny, but she hadn't expected to be driving much, and certainly not the first day she arrived.

After practicing in the parking lot for half an hour, she'd felt secure enough to venture out onto the roads, clutching a map with bewildering names she couldn't pronounce. Then she and a mailbox (how was she supposed to know where the left side of her car was when she was busy trying to avoid the dratted sheep that kept *catapulting* themselves onto the road?) had gotten into a bit of a tussle. At thirty-five hours, and counting, without sleep she'd been offering her Visa to an elderly and amused man with a thick burr, who'd shrugged it off, pointed her in the right direction, and told her she was nearly at the MacKeltar castle.

Castle? Life had taken on distinct *Twilight Zone* qualities.

Seventeen long-haired sheep ambling straight down the center of the road as if they owned it (possession being nine-tenths of the law, she was hardly in a position to argue, though she'd certainly shouted enough nasty things out the window) and thirty minutes of a thick, swirling snowfall later, she'd slipped into the icy drive of the MacKeltar castle, shaking with exhaustion.

It was nearly ten in the evening.

Smoothing a hand over the small portion of hair that remained plaited, she forced herself to get out of the car. She lugged her luggage up the steps, then stopped and tipped her head back, gazing up at the castle. Snow dusted her cheeks and lips, then melted swiftly on her tongue as her jaw dropped gently.

Castle, indeed.

Even nearly dead on her feet, she wasn't immune to the centuries-old stone structure's beauty. Towering above her, the sprawling wings stretched east and west from the central hall, disappearing into the darkness. She pivoted in a slow circle, taking it all in. Majestic snow-covered hills shimmered like pearls beneath a round, white moon. The road she'd taken up to the castle was already covered with fresh snow, concealing her tracks. A few more inches of drift, and a person wouldn't even know a road was there. Not a single man-made noise could be heard, not one car engine or horn honking, no stereo blasting from a nearby apartment complex.

Eerie. But soothing.

She was stricken by a sudden chill and quickly tugged the zipper of her parka up to her neck, but the chill seemed a deeper thing, in her bones, as if Scotland might somehow change her before she managed to find her way out again.

"Och, dearie, we're so sorry!" Maeve Jameson exclaimed for the third time, wringing her ring-bedecked hands.

"Sure as the sun sets, we forgot," Nigel Jameson, Maeve's husband, added sheepishly, whisking off Elisabeth's parka and pushing her into a deep armchair near a blazing fire.

The couple, both gray-haired and in their early sixties, had been fussing and fretting and apologizing since the moment she'd stepped out of the blustery wind and into the honest-to-goodness Greathall. Into the honest-to-goodness sprawling castle that had corridors shooting off in all direction and must have had a hundred rooms or more.

Within moments she was clutching a steaming cup of

cocoa, courtesy of Nigel, while Maeve bustled back and forth between hall and kitchen, laying cold cuts and cheese, thick, gold-crusted bread, a creamy potato salad, and a tray of condiments on the small table beside her.

"Forgive us, dearie, but it's been such a day. You have no idea. What with the terrible accident on our minds—"

"And then with the sheep gettin' oot, and us busy trying to round 'em up again—" Nigel said.

"And with Gwen being pregnant and all—"

"And the laird having a concussion—"

"Concussion? Pregnant? Did you say accident?" Elisabeth exclaimed, struggling to digest the bits of conversation that were alarmingly vague. "Can you start at the beginning?"

"Well, we plumb forgot to meet you at the airport," Nigel said, as if that explained everything.

"What accident?" Elisabeth asked, hoping she hadn't just invited another mad rush of vague half sentences.

Maeve sank into a chair beside her, fussing nervously with her short, curly hair. "The laird and lady were in Edinburgh yesterday when some biddle-brained American—sorry, not meaning any offense, dearie—was driving on the wrong side of the road and hit the MacKeltars head on. And being as Gwen's six months pregnant—"

"She is? She didn't tell me that when we spoke on the phone." Nor had Gwen bothered to mention that she'd married a bona fide lord and lived in a castle. Heavens, they had a lot of catching up to do! Gwen had also been reticent to discuss her brother-in-law's condition, promising they'd speak about it when Elisabeth arrived.

"Aye," Nigel said, beaming. "Twins."

"Is Gwen all right?" Elisabeth worried. "The babies?"

Nigel nodded. "No broken bones and the wee bairns are fine, but she got knocked about a bit, so they're after keeping her for a time to be certain all's well."

"And Drustan's concussed, with no few scrapes and bruises."

"So it seems they may not be back 'til the end of the week and then when the sheep got oot—"

"What with the boys being off to London for a wee holiday—"

"Well, as you can see we've had our hands full—"

"Which is no excuse, but—"

"Begging your forgiveness, we are," Nigel said earnestly, and Maeve nodded.

Elisabeth took a slow, deep breath. "I see," she said, waiting cautiously to see if they were going to burst into another simultaneous conversation.

But they didn't. Merely sat, regarding her expectantly.

"Oh," she said hastily, realizing they were waiting for her to accept their apology. "Don't worry about it. I got here just fine," she lied. "No problem at all."

They beamed.

"That's a fine thing, then," Maeve said. "Drink up, drink up, 'tis a brisk night for the bones. Once you have a bite to eat, we'll settle you in your chambers."

Elisabeth took a few sips of her cocoa, trying to gather her wits, but they'd long since trundled off to sleep without her consent. "My patient?" she managed to ask. She'd like to know something about him before she went to bed, so she'd be better prepared to meet him in the morning. She hoped he wasn't expecting to meet her this evening. She was far too exhausted to make a professional impression.

Maeve and Nigel exchanged a long glance. "You mean the laird's brother, Dageus?" Nigel asked carefully.

Elisabeth nodded.

"No need to fash yourself o'er him for the now," Nigel said. "When the laird returns, he'll take you to meet him."

"You mean he's not here? He doesn't live in the castle?" Elisabeth asked, surprised.

They shook their heads in tandem.

"Well, where is he?"

Another long glance was exchanged. "In a cottage," Nigel said.

"North of the castle," Maeve added.

"By himself?" Elisabeth asked, mildly shocked. It wasn't good for a person suffering mental problems, even if only a case of depression, to live alone. Isolation was never conducive to recovery.

"Aye."

"And he's, er . . . fine living by himself?" she pressed, hoping they'd volunteer a useful bit of information. Though she wouldn't sink to interrogating Gwen's hired help, she certainly would like to know something about the man before she met him.

"Aye."

"S'ppose so."

Elisabeth cocked her head, studying the Jamesons curiously. The loquacious couple had dwindled down to one- and two-word answers. Most peculiar. "I'll just go introduce myself in the morning."

"No!" they both shouted.

Elisabeth blinked.

"I mean, that is to say the laird bid you wait until he returned," Nigel said hastily. "Then he'll be taking you to meet him proper-like."

"All right," Elisabeth said warily, puzzled by their reaction. Then, after a few moments of uncomfortable silence, it occurred to her that if the Jamesons and "the boys" were the sole caretakers of the vast estate, and the boys were away, the elderly couple probably didn't have time to take on a single extra responsibility. Likely, they were worrying about just how they might keep her occupied until Gwen and Drustan returned. Well, she wouldn't be a bother to them, she resolved sleepily. She could find north just fine by herself.

Maeve smiled uncertainly. "There you are, then. Eat up and we'll see about tucking you in for the night. You must be fair weary from traveling."

You have no idea, Elisabeth thought.

So bone-weary in fact, that when she stumbled into bed thirty minutes later, she'd didn't even pause to undress, but fell asleep with her parka and boots still on.

4

DAGEUS MACKELTAR WAS DREAMING.

In his dream, he stood in the circle of the powerful Ban Drochaid stones beneath a vast and velvety night sky. Gàidhlig for "white bridge," the Ban Drochaid was just that—a bridge through time for a man privy to the arcane and dangerous knowledge.

He'd already etched the thirteen complex formulas on the thirteen stones. Now he need but complete the final three on the center slab to open a gate through time.

It was five minutes to midnight on Yule, the winter solstice, the year 1521. It was one of the final times that he'd been in his beloved sixteenth-century Highlands.

His brother, Drustan, was dead. And grief and guilt were eating him alive.

Three years earlier, Dageus had made a pledge to Gwen;

that he would protect her and all those she loved. Protect them with his life if necessary.

He'd failed. And now Drustan would never be reunited with his wife in the twenty-first century. Gwen would never see her husband again. Would she wait and grieve and die a little inside each day? he brooded. Should he send her a message down through the centuries? *We tried, but I failed and he died.*

Nay, Dageus knew what action he must take. It was his fault that Drustan had died. He'd not been home the night the fire had taken Drustan's life. If he had, he would have stopped the fire before it had gutted the tower in which his brother lay slumbering.

But he'd not been there because he'd been in the bed of a lass whose name he couldn't even recall, sick to death of watching Silvan and Nell, so in love and busy with their new babes. Sick to death of imagining Gwen and Drustan's joy when at long last they reunited. Sick to death of being alone. Of having his twin brother who'd been his best friend since the moment they'd drawn breath, sleeping in the next room, where he would sleep until long after Dageus had died.

Seeking the bed of a lass so he could pretend for a time that he had a place and a woman of his own.

Drustan had always known exactly who he was and where he fit. When he chose a course, he never faltered. But Dageus faltered. He'd faltered when he'd wanted to marry his fair Brea, and he was faltering now.

'Tis an old custom, he'd promised Gwen. *I shall always protect you and yours . . . I owe you my life.*

By Amergin, the least he could do was keep his word! He had mere minutes to sketch the final symbols. He could go back in time to the day of the fire and prevent it from happening. Keep Drustan from dying. Ascertain that he and his wife were reunited. Eyes narrowed, he studied the night sky. Two minutes.

But the legend . . .

He shook his head, rejecting the notion. 'Twas but a fae tale told to strike fear into the hearts of those who kept the coveted secret of the stones. There were no evil druids trapped in some in-between place, waiting to claim a Keltar who broke his oath. Nor was there any record of a MacKeltar having so much as glimpsed a Tuatha Dé Danann for millennia. The ancient tomes that mentioned them referred in vague terms to a vaguer race. Who knew if they still existed, if indeed they had?

Likely as not, he told himself, the legend was naught more than a myth told and retold—and getting taller in the telling—to prevent a Keltar from using the stones indiscriminately.

He had no intention of using them indiscriminately.

He'd thought his decision through long and hard. He wasn't using the stones for personal motive. Love had to be singularly the most selfless motive in the world. Beyond all Druid powers, beyond the mysterious and fascinating heavens, beyond death, was not love the purest and most precious thing?

Mayhap he was destined never to know the kind of love Drustan shared with Gwen, but it *was* in his power to ascertain that his brother shared a long life of loving with his wife.

He must have etched the final symbols while lost in thought, for he had little memory of it, dreaming or waking. But the white bridge opened, and then it was too late for regret.

Dageus's mind shattered as dimensions altered. Time unfurled into a thing of strange symmetry and exhilarating beauty, stretching, bending, and curving. He felt free and as immense as the universe. Understanding crashed over him, an understanding of the laws of nature that had always danced just beyond his reach. He was awed. He was humbled. He was filled with an incredible feeling of connectedness, a flawless perception of his place in the world . . .

Until everything went terribly wrong.

Screeching and howling like a pack of banshees, they fell on him.

A storm ripped open the night, lightning stabbed at the earth, and hail rained down in bruising torrents. But the storm without his body was naught compared to the storm within: They surrounded him, they clawed at him. They *became* him.

He howled mindlessly as, shrieking their ancient names and ancient demands, they filled his head with a deafening cacophony.

Then there was darkness so complete he doubted he would ever find his way out again.

———

Dageus woke with a violent start. He'd had the dream again, and by Amergin, he'd relived that choice a thousand times, yet had only to see Gwen and Drustan together to know that he'd made the right one. But sometimes, in the wee hours of the morn when his cottage in the vale was cloaked in utter silence and he felt like the only man alive, he lay awake and wondered what his life might have been otherwise.

What it still can *be* . . . the eldest of the thirteen, Droghda reminded. *You speak as if life is o'er when yours has but begun.*

Let us teach you our ways. We have power, power you've ne'er dreamed of. Let us make you invincible . . .

Then twelve other voices joined in, making threats and promises. Insisting that the Tuatha Dé Danann had lied to the Keltar, had cheated them of their full powers. The noise inside his head swiftly grew deafening.

Cursing, he pushed himself up from the tangled bed linens, but collapsed to the floor. He clamped his hands to his ears in a wholly instinctive and wholly futile gesture. The attack had come quickly this time, and it took him several long moments before he managed to force himself up from the floor. He collapsed again, but slowly managed to turn the battle into push-ups. He pumped up and down, again and again, until his body ran with sweat. Until his heart hammered, until he could hear naught but the blood pounding in his veins. Then he started on stomach crunches.

When at last the voices faded and his mind was calm again, Dageus fell back on the floor, sweating and breathing hard. He smiled bitterly. It was ironic that he'd be at his strongest, in peak physical condition, when he died.

Thus far, he'd discovered three ways to control the voices inside his head: tupping, his personal favorite; performing Druid magic, large or small, as all things Druid pleased his tormentors; and prolonged, strenuous physical exertion.

It was the former and the latter that were of great use. He'd discovered that tupping helped while he'd passed a bewildering month in twenty-first-century Edinburgh waiting for Drustan to awaken. There, he'd also discovered that women had much greater freedom to take lovers than had lasses in the sixteenth century, where a missing maidenhead might topple the succession of a clan.

The second method of silencing the thirteen, performing Druid magic, was dangerous. When he'd first come through the stones, confounded by the new century, he'd used the Druid voice of power to procure food and shelter until he'd bartered gold coins and two of his blades for modern currency. Aye, magic stilled the thirteen, yet the few times he'd used it, they'd been stronger when they'd surfaced again. Louder, clearer of mind. How he was loath to use even the tiniest spell.

Exercise and tupping silenced them completely, and sometimes the blessed silence lasted as long as a day. It was Gwen who'd suggested exercise. Gwen believed that mayhap tupping and exercise released a chemical combination in his body that had a sedating effect on the ancient beings.

Tupping was no longer an option, since he was trapped in the valley, and naught but bleating sheep ever trundled by, so exercise had become his salvation. Dageus didn't pretend to understand the how or why of it, he merely knew that for now it worked.

He also knew that the thirteen learned swiftly, adapted at an alarming rate. He fully expected they would, in time, find a way to overcome his methods of silencing them. Dageus hoped he didn't live to see that day.

Of late, he wearied of living to see *any* day. On the rare occasions he managed to sleep through the night, the morn brought only the sure knowledge that the blackness within him had grown whilst he slumbered.

And, och, but the blackness was becoming seductive, offering an end to the guilt and despair and self-recrimination. He wondered what it might be like to plunge headlong into it. To exult in the power and freedom they offered.

And he knew that meant time was running out. When the thirteen had first entered him, they'd been crazed from thousands of years of imprisonment. They'd been unfocused, seeming unaware that they'd regained a measure of freedom, and uncertain what to do with it.

But that uncertainty hadn't lasted long. The night Drustan had brought him back to MacKeltar land, the Ban Drochaid stones had called out to him, singing with an energy that hummed throughout his body. Places of power and magic beckoned him as never before. He'd tried to walk past the stones, into the castle, but had been unable to take a single step, for he'd known if he had, he would have walked straight into the center of the circle and grown drunk on power.

That very night Christopher and Drustan had trapped him in the cottage. In his vale he was far enough from the stones that they were but a soft fire in his blood, not a consuming blaze.

Day by day the thirteen grew stronger, urging him to go back to their time, back further than he could fathom. Back to the time of the legendary Tuatha Dé Danann, and to a fateful battle hinted at only vaguely in Keltar myth. Although the thirteen were inside him, he was not privy to their thoughts—unless they chose to communicate them—any more than they were to his. Yet, of late, in dreams, the boundaries between he and the thirteen were blurring, and he feared that he might one day awaken and be unable to subdue them. That he might awaken irrevocably changed. He'd confided this fear to Drustan, but Drustan had refused to hear it, refused to admit even the possibility of it.

It was the bitter thought that he might disappoint his brother again that gave him strength to fight each day. He need only hold them at bay long enough that Drustan and Christopher could find a way to end his life without releasing the dark Druids into the world, or worse, into someone else. The problem was they didn't know what laws governed the non-corporeal beings and, to date, had found naught of use in the ancient tomes.

And it wasn't as if he could ask the thirteen. They'd not participate willingly in their own destruction. Nay, they'd fight to the bitter end. He'd learned that lesson all too well the night he'd tried to end his own life. The instant he'd pressed the blade to his breast, the thirteen had exploded in a cacophony of voices, urging him to do it because then, they told him, they would be released into the world. The ancient Druid art of transmigration, they'd howled, would allow them to take anyone's body. *So kill yourself,* they'd shrieked. *Set us free.*

He had no way of knowing whether it was true. If indeed they could transmigrate. He'd begun to suspect that the Tuatha Dé Danann's Druids were a vastly different breed than the Keltar Druids, possessing far greater powers. And far fewer misgivings about using it.

He dare not risk it. The thirteen could not be permitted to claim an innocent life. No other man, woman, or child would be made to pay for his mistakes.

He'd dropped the blade and wept then, for the first and final time.

And now he lived to accomplish but one thing.

To die with that precious commodity he'd so utterly failed to live with: honor.

5

ELISABETH GOT UP EARLY THE NEXT MORNING, DETERMINED to slip out without disturbing the Jamesons, so they wouldn't feel obligated to take time away from their chores. She wasn't about to be a burden to the elderly couple. Nor was she about to waste a week waiting for Gwen and Drustan to return. Happiest when working, she was eager to begin her first official assignment. And eager to prove to herself that the man didn't really look like the picture he'd painted. She would introduce herself (informally, for today, so they might grow comfortable with each other), identify his "problem," and devise a plan of treatment.

Elisabeth showered quickly and dressed for the wintry clime in jeans, hiking boots, a thick woolen sweater, parka, ski cap, and mittens, then went downstairs.

She hurried to the front door and was about to open it when she heard Nigel shouting out by the road, followed by loud, defiant bleating. Surmising that the sheep must be on another of their peculiar rampages, she pivoted and hurried down the nearest corridor until she realized she was subconsciously following the smell of coffee. From the sound of pots and pans banging about, Maeve was already up and in the kitchen. That wouldn't do. Both of them clearly had their hands full.

Striking back in the opposite direction, she poked her head into room after room, until she finally discovered the French doors in the study that opened off the rear of the castle.

Hoping Maeve had a good sense of direction, Elisabeth used the sun to orient herself and struck off on a northerly route, telling herself she didn't really need a cup of coffee. The frigid walk across the snowy hills and valleys would wake her up just fine.

And it did. The beauty alone, if not the frigid breath-stealing wind, would have shocked her into full consciousness. She could see for miles in every direction. The sun streaked the morning sky with red and gold. Off in the distance, atop a far mountain, sprawled another castle strikingly similar to the MacKeltars'. Squinting, she could make out the silhouettes of standing stones against the rosy morning sky. She eyed them, wondering if that castle might be where her patient had done his self-portrait.

Nearly an hour later, cupping a mitten over her frozen nose, and seriously doubting that Maeve knew north from a hole in her head, Elisabeth was about to turn back when she topped a steep hill and spied the cottage, nestled snugly in the immense snowy valley below. She paused, catching her breath and admiring the picture it made, surrounded by sparkling, snow-covered hills.

Constructed of stone, it faced east and was simplicity itself, cozy and delightfully inviting. Twelve tall windows, six on each floor, reflected the brilliant sun. Snow blanketed the sloping roof, dropping from the edges, landing on bush-shaped mounds below. Glittering icicles hung from the eaves. *And oh, joy of joys,* she thought, clenching her teeth to keep them from chattering, no less than four chimneys were puffing merrily away. Perhaps she could thaw her fingers and toes by a fire. He might even offer her something hot to drink.

Harvard suddenly seemed light-years away, with its bustle and competitiveness and brittle gloss, and she was puzzled by the sense of relief she suddenly felt. Maybe she was just long overdue for a vacation, she decided. Gazing down at the vast valley, unmarred by any sign of modern technology, she could imagine what the Scotland of yore had been like, with miles and miles of unspoiled beauty. She found the stillness and old-fashioned simplicity oddly captivating. As if she could breathe easier in these clean, untamed mountains.

Tugging her hat more snugly over her ears, she hastened down the hill toward the cottage. She was curious about Dageus MacKeltar, had been since the moment she'd laid eyes on his painting. Gwen's reluctance to discuss him on the phone had only heightened her curiosity.

It had made her a bit anxious as well. She reminded herself that since he was well enough to live alone, he probably had nothing more than a case of depression that would nicely fit the classic theories.

She imagined his body language would be defensive and

closed. He might fold his arms and cross and uncross his legs, or make only brief eye contact before his gaze skittered away. He would be eager to talk, yet defiant. And he would look nothing like that idiotic painting. A kilt, indeed! *Short, over-weight, and balding,* she reminded herself.

Carefully navigating the drifts blanketing the front lawn, she hurried to the door of the cottage, her breath frosting the air. She was leaning forward, her hand fisted to knock, when the door was pulled abruptly inward. Off balance, she stumbled. Flailing for the doorjamb, she barely managed to keep herself from falling flat on her face.

The moment during which she raised her gaze from the threshold to his bare chest seemed to take years. There was just too much golden, glistening skin poured over muscle, and too little clothing for a girl's comfort. By the time her gaze hit his chin, her breathing was shallow and irregular.

Oh, please God, no, she thought, her hopes crashing to her toes as she craned her neck to stare up at him.

Oh, thank you, God, yes, her id breathed reverently, all but genuflecting.

As if he'd simply stepped right out of the painting, sans kilt, there he stood.

Not short, in fact, he towered over her. Not fat, there wasn't a spare ounce on him. Just ripples and velvety skin and . . . power. And definitely not balding, she thought, staring at thick, silky black hair pulled back at his nape.

He exuded every bit as much presence and raw sensuality as he had on canvas. The man was positively magnetic. She fancied her hair might be crackling with static electricity from the energy rolling off him. The painting hadn't *begun* to do him justice. His face was exquisitely masculine, exquisitely sensual, his cheekbones and jaw chiseled in stark relief by a dusting of a shadow beard. His lips were firm and full, and she got all hung up there for a moment. Only with immense effort did she force herself to meet his eyes.

They were golden. Shimmery, exotic amber, tempered with darker flecks.

She stared. The beauty of the man had completely numbed her brain. Either that or she'd been hiking way too long.

He stared right back.

"You're no' a sheep," he said finally, in a husky Scots burr.

"No," she agreed breathlessly, stupidly, unable to dredge up a single intelligent thing to say. Like her name. Or hello. Or even, Gee, isn't there a lot of snow?

"'Tis but that I've seen naught but sheep for some time now," he clarified, staring.

"You're not, er . . . dressed," she stammered, struggling valiantly to keep her gaze from dropping to his toes and back up again.

"I'm no' naked." A long pause. Then huskily, "But I could remedy that, lass."

Elisabeth gaped at him, trying to decide if he meant to remedy it by dressing or undressing, and lost a few moments imagining him completely nude. It took an icicle, melting in the morning sun, falling from the eave above her head, and shattering into brittle shards on the ground between them, to jar her back to reality.

They both jerked like startled sleepwalkers and thrust out their hands.

"I'm Elisabeth."

"Dageus," he said, catching her hand quickly, and raising it to his lips.

"Zanders." She snatched her hand away before those dangerous lips could so much as brush her skin.

"MacKeltar." He arched a brow and something flared in his eyes. A hint of laughter? A brush of cockiness? A subtle challenge sensed? She hoped not. He looked like the kind of man who tackled challenges with brutal enthusiasm.

"Come in, lass," he purred, opening the door wide, never taking his eyes off her. "I've not had a wom—er, visitor in the longest time."

Elisabeth took a deep breath that was supposed to be calming, but it didn't help. Despite her best intentions, her gaze dropped from his face to his muscled, sweat-glistening chest. Ever the student of body language, an invaluable tool in her profession, and cursing herself for it at the moment, she observed that his nipples were hard. *The cold,* she translated, struggling for detachment. *It's the combination of sweat and cold.*

And yours are hard why? her id queried smugly.

She flushed, grateful for her bulky parka. Before her gaze could drop any lower, and start skimming those black gym shorts to check for other body language she oh-so-definitely had no business checking for, she closed her eyes. *This just won't do at all, Zanders. Get a grip.*

"Och, lass, I've embarrassed you," he apologized, without one ounce of apology in his voice. "Come in. I'll be naught more than a moment getting dressed," he said in a thick burr. It was a strange accent, unlike Maeve's or Nigel's. Unlike any she'd heard in Scotland so far.

"Perhaps I should come back l-later," she stammered, opening her eyes. Big mistake. Her gaze began a slow slide straight back down his body again as, much to her consternation, he watched her, and the corner of his sensual mouth lifted in a faint smile. "It was foolish of me t-to . . ." *come unannounced* was what she was trying to get out, but she trailed off when he closed a hand around her upper arm, yanked her inside, and closed the door behind her.

He braced his palms against the door, on either side of her head, walling her in with six-feet-plus of glistening, gorgeous male flesh.

For a long, awful moment, Elisabeth thought the man was going to kiss her. Just duck his head and cover her lips with his and—oh, for a long, awful moment she could nearly taste it. Taste things that only existed between the covers of a fantasy novel. Fortunately, despite her traitorous inner thoughts, she must have looked horrified, because when he searched her face intently, something flared in his eyes, and he dropped his hands and eased back a step.

As if he'd decided not to terrify her too much. Yet.

"My home is yours, lass," he said softly in his thick burr. "Bide a wee with me and shake your chill. Would you be liking tea? Nay," he amended swiftly, "I'm thinking you're American. It'll be coffee, will it no'?"

"Coffee would be lovely," she managed, averting her gaze and trying to regain a measure of calm by cataloging her surroundings.

To her right was a colorful, sunny room filled with lush plants, free weights, benches, and pads, and an elliptical crosstrainer. Classical music was playing softly, from multiple speakers. To her left was a living room with a bright blaze crackling in the fireplace. She eyed the plush sofa, the books scattered about, the television, the marble-topped tables, and the empty wineglasses, anything but him. *Come on, Zanders, get it together,* she chided herself. *This man is supposed to be our patient.*

Then we're in trouble with a capital T, she thought grimly.

How dare he be so heart-stoppingly male? Was it too much to ask that she might have gotten a normal, midlife-crisis-having, bespectacled, balding patient on her first premature lunge from the gates? She glared at him but he'd somehow gotten behind her and was herding her down a hallway into the kitchen, a cozy room hung with drying herbs and gleaming copper-bottomed pans and yet another fire.

"Then sit, lass," he said, right behind her ear. She realized, much to her chagrin, that she'd just been very effectively manipulated. He'd neither invited her into the kitchen, nor taken her along by the elbow. In fact, he'd not touched her at all. He'd merely used the presence of his warm, nearly naked body in her personal space, to direct her where he wanted her to go. Like a dog herding sheep. And like a witless sheep, she'd trundled obediently along.

Oh, definitely trouble with a capital T.

His breath was warm near her ear, his voice husky. "Toast your toes by the fire, lass. I'll be after a shirt and trews, then see to brewing some coffee."

When he stepped away from her and left the room, she could have sworn her body temperature dropped several degrees. She'd stopped feeling chilled from her snowy trek the moment he'd opened the door. But when he'd stood close behind her, she felt flushed, nearly feverish.

She stared out the window, trying to collect herself. She folded her hands in her lap and took slow deep breaths.

Elisabeth had never reacted to a man the way she reacted to Dageus MacKeltar. Oh, she'd dated a few men, even fooled around a bit. Once, she'd even gone pretty far. But not all the way. Perhaps, she acknowledged ruefully, she'd never gone all the way only because she'd never felt anything like this before. A desperate, immediate physical attraction that—because it had caught her so off guard—had muddled her senses completely. For a moment she'd been only a woman, and he only a man.

And that just wouldn't do.

Now that she knew what to expect, she assured herself, she'd be able to control it. Being attracted to one's patient violated the cardinal rule of therapy. *Face it, Zanders, it's either the man, or lots of money.* She knew which one had greater staying power, despite him looking like the poster boy for stamina.

Money was real. Career was real. People, well, people had a bad habit of disappearing just when one needed them the most.

———

Dageus watched her over his shoulder as he toweled the sweat from his body and stepped into a pair of loose-fitting black trews. If she made one move toward the door, he was fair certain he would tackle her. But she didn't. She sat stiffly at the kitchen table, hands folded neatly in her lap, staring fixedly out the west window at the frozen pond.

He made her nervous, he thought. Good.

She made him hard as a rock. He could scarce believe she

was there. A woman. Lush and lovely. Sitting at his table. About to have coffee with him.

He'd been doing sit-ups in the sunroom when he'd glanced outside and seen the lass headed straight for his door. He'd not clapped eyes upon a woman other than Gwen in four months. He'd stopped mid crunch and stared, stunned, as she'd clambered over the deep drifts that covered the front lawn. Coming right toward him—an innocent sheep ambling straight for the wolf. And as a wolf might lick his chops, he'd wet his lips, his body tensing, his blood quickening.

She was a bonny lass, wee like Gwen, and, in his estimation, even lovelier. But he wanted to do something about all that curly hair she'd trapped so snugly beneath her blue woolen cap. Set it free. Bury his hands in it. Tendrils of silver and honey had escaped her cap and curled about her cold-flushed cheeks. Her stormy blue eyes were huge beneath delicately arched brows. Her skin was smooth, translucent as pearl. Her upper lip was slightly fuller than her lower and uptilted. Pure, sinful temptation that mouth was, he thought, his eyes narrowing as he imagined what he'd like to do with it. Although her bulky parka camouflaged the curves of her body, her shapely legs clad in denim trews hinted at a lush figure. He ached to peel off the layers of her clothing, drag her to his bed, and keep her there until neither of them could move. He envisioned her luscious lips parted on a whimper of pleasure as he buried himself deeply inside her.

What vagary of fate had brought her to his door? he wondered, tugging a T-shirt over his head. He took several deep breaths, willing his man parts to stop tenting the fabric of his trews. When that didn't work, he rearranged himself, and untucked his shirt.

It tented, too.

Exasperated, he fastened his sporran around his waist. There were sound reasons Scotsmen wore the things so often—and who could traipse about in naught but a kilt otherwise? He didn't understand how modern-day men managed without them.

The moment his eyes met hers, they'd both tensed like startled animals. An experienced man, he'd recognized it for mating heat, and of an uncommon intensity at that. But there was something else, too, something . . . deeper.

Och, and for sure the lass found him attractive. She'd all but eaten him up with her eyes.

He rubbed his jaw thoughtfully. Gwen and Drustan wouldn't be back for days. He was fine with keeping the lovely visitor for himself for a time. Rather like a dying man's last supper. And blethering hell, the lass was a veritable feast.

6

WHEN DAGEUS RETURNED TO THE KITCHEN, THE LASS startled, then gave him a stiff smile.

"I'm sorry," she said quickly. "I'm not usually so clumsy. I just wasn't expecting someone to open the door at that moment and I was off balance."

So that was the way she would play it, Dageus thought, amused. Pretend a flash of pure fire hadn't passed between them. Pretend she'd done nothing more than stumble at his doorstep. He'd permit it. For a time. "I'm sorry I startled you, lass," he gave her the words she wanted to hear.

He turned his back to her and busied himself retrieving beans from the freezer, putting them in a grinder, and grinding them to a fine powder. Not the imported *cofaidh* he'd grown fond of in Edinburgh, but it would do. He let the silence between them spin out, curious to see what she would do with it. Would she *haver* away, filling the space betwixt them with nervous chatter?

"As I was saying, I'm Elisabeth Zanders," she said after a long moment, with a false note of brightness.

Aye, she would *haver*. "I caught your name the first time, lass."

"And as you know, Gwen asked me to come," she chirped.

Dageus nearly dropped the carafe at that. He knew no such thing. He placed the carafe carefully on the counter before turning to face her. "Indeed," he said slowly. *Gwen* had sent her? Was he dreaming?

She nodded encouragingly. "I'm here to help you," she said gently.

To help him? Och, by Amergin, the gods were smiling on him! This was the last thing he would have expected of Gwen!

But all of a sudden, a recent conversation he'd had with Gwen when she'd last visited him made more sense. She'd mentioned several times that she disliked him being alone so much. She'd worried that it wasn't good for him. She'd seemed to be hinting around at something, but had left without disclosing what had been on her mind, as if the subject had been too uncomfortable for her to broach.

This was it then. She'd devised a solution to his loneliness. And yet another way to keep the thirteen in check. With a whore, bought and paid for. Although he'd ne'er have expected it of her, it was, he admitted, a tidy solution. He rubbed his jaw, pondering the fascinating development.

"With your problems," Elisabeth continued, with another of those little nods.

"Um-hmm." He eyed her leisurely from head to toe, digesting his bonny fortune. Thinking how he would savor peeling off layer after layer of her clothing.

"I know you might find it difficult to relax with a perfect stranger—"

"Not at all, lass," he said silkily.

"—but I think you'll find I'm a good listener."

Listener? He'd liked his women making noise and a lot of it, not listening.

"So I thought we could start tomorrow, and just get comfortable with each other today."

Still trying to assimilate that the lass had been sent by Gwen to share his bed, Dageus turned back to the coffeemaker and finished preparing it in silence.

It felt odd to him, he realized. Although he desired her intensely, and had only moments before been planning her seduction, he didn't care for her speaking of such things so casually. It chafed his pride. It chafed what remained of his heart.

But not so much that he'd send the lass away. Nay, nowhere near that much.

"I see no reason to wait until tomorrow," he said, coming to a swift decision. His entire body was tense with wanting. He'd been four months without a woman, and this one turned his blood to fire. Once he'd bedded her he'd wager she'd not again speak so casually of *helping him*. Nay, he'd tup her 'til she melted into a dreamy-eyed lass, and free that wild-haired creature he suspected lurked just beneath the proper surface. Then *he'd* help *her*. To a full measure of carnal bliss. And she'd stay with him because she wanted to—not because she'd been paid to do so. Dageus might be certain of little else

of late, but he was unequivocally certain of his expertise with
the lasses. When he'd lost his fair Brea, he'd devoted himself
to learning everything there was to know about pleasuring a
woman, certain that if he'd been better, if he'd been able to
make it for her the way it had felt to him, she'd have waited
for him. No matter how long it had taken.

"Are you certain? I mean, you feel comfortable with me
already?" She beamed up at him, looking inordinately
pleased by the thought.

"Och, aye, lass," he said, feeling inexplicably irritable.
"More than comfortable enough to tup."

"Toop?" she echoed blankly, her smile wobbling a bit.

"Er . . ." Dageus rummaged about for another word from
her century that she might be more familiar with, and seized
the vernacular he'd picked up recently. The word had con-
fused him at first, being used for such a variety of reasons.
"Fuck," he clarified.

The smile fell right off her face, and she blanched. "F-
F— Oh! Who said anything about *th-that*?" She snapped so
abruptly straight in her chair that it clattered against the
stone floor and nearly toppled over.

He blinked, startled by her reaction. "You did."

"I did *not*!"

"You did too," he said patiently.

"Oh, absolutely not!" she practically shouted.

Dageus blinked. "There's no need to shout the roof down
about my ears, lass."

"There is if you think I came here to-to—" she broke off,
sputtering. She skittered backward in her chair, scooting it
bumpily across the stone floor. "Just because I gawked at you
doesn't mean I-I—" she broke off again, cheeks flaming.

Dageus studied her closely. She looked shocked, appalled, and mildly guilty. "Have I misunderstood you, lass?" he asked carefully. "You said Gwen sent you. Why did she send you to my home?"

"To *talk* to you! To *talk* about your problems! I'm a *psychologist*!"

Psychologist? Puzzling over the strange word, one of hundreds he'd encountered during his time in the twenty-first century, he deconstructed it into base parts: psyche and logos—a study of the mind? Gwen had sent some wee young lass to study his mind? What the blethering hell did she think that might accomplish? Disappointment that he wouldn't be bedding her (at least not at the moment, he thought, with dark amusement) mingled with pure relief that she wasn't bought and paid for. He hadn't liked thinking of her, or "tooping," as a commodity bought and paid for. Ne'er had Dageus MacKeltar exchanged coin for bed play. He'd not liked the feel of it.

Then the absurdity of his foolish assumption struck him, and he made a choking noise, trying to swallow a burst of laughter. *When a lass is fashed, a wise man doesn't laugh,* his da, Silvan, had oft reminded him. Such advice had long stood Dageus in good stead with women.

Och, what a fool he'd been, thinking Gwen had sent him a woman to warm his bed! *This* was what Gwen had been hinting at during her last visit. That she'd be sending him some modern-day mind studier for him to *talk* to. *Talk, my arse,* he thought, eyes narrowing. *Talk her naked, mayhap.*

"Why did you *think* I was here?" she said stiffly.

"If you haven't figured that out, lass, leave be," he warned, rubbing his jaw to hide the smile he couldn't quite tame. Nay, definitely not bought and paid for. Spitting furious with him at the moment. And lovely as could be, all temper-flushed and sparkly eyed.

"Oh, I've figured it out. And I don't believe for a minute," she hissed, "that Gwen would send someone to you for *that*."

"Verily, upon reflection neither do I, but 'twas a rather glorious moment while I did," he said easily.

Elisabeth scowled at him, firmly ignoring the tiny voice inside her that was saying, *"A glorious moment?" Me? Really?* The thought that a man like him might consider her a glorious moment did funny things to her stomach.

His eyes were glittering with amusement and he looked like he was trying not to laugh. If he did, she was afraid she might throw something at him. The man didn't possess an ounce of civilized embarrassment. He should be mortified, not calmly admitting that he'd found the thought of doing *that* with her glorious.

And that word! When he'd said that word, it had sent a jolt of pure energy to her, er . . . parts of herself she shouldn't be thinking about. She'd been terrified that she'd made a classic Freudian slip. Mentally reviewing their conversation, she hadn't been able to isolate just how or when, but it had definitely been on her mind, and what woman wouldn't be thinking such things while looking at him?

A professional, Zanders, which you clearly are not.

How on earth was she going to regain control of the situation?

"Has Gwen ever sent a woman to you for such a thing before?" Elisabeth asked tersely, wondering if she really knew Gwen as well as she thought.

"Nay," he replied smoothly. "But you know how newly

wedded couples are. They think everyone should be experiencing the joys of wedded bliss. Gwen has been trying to matchmake for me, and I merely thought you were her latest effort. There you were saying you wanted me to relax and get to know you, and I thought you were, er . . . an unusually forward lass."

"Didn't Gwen tell you I was arriving yesterday?" Elisabeth asked, frowning. Perhaps Gwen had neglected to mention his psychologist's gender, and he'd been expecting a man.

He shook his head.

A sudden, terrible thought occurred to her, a thought that positively made her cringe. Reluctantly, she voiced it. "Mr. MacKeltar, did you know that Gwen had hired me to work with you?"

He shook his head. "Nay. Verily, she ne'er mentioned a word of it."

"You didn't have any idea that she'd hired a psychologist for you?" Elisabeth repeated, as if rephrasing it slightly might make him change his answer to the one she wanted to hear.

He didn't. "Nay," he replied. "Nor have I any need of one, lass."

Elisabeth closed her eyes, stunned, belatedly understanding why Gwen had wanted her to wait until she returned from the hospital. She'd assumed from Gwen's letter that Dageus MacKeltar knew Gwen was arranging professional help for him. She'd *assumed*.

And you know what assuming does, her id needled, *makes an ass out of u and me.*

She groaned inwardly. A man like him probably had a different woman throwing herself at him every day of the week and two on Sundays. It wasn't as if she'd shown up on his doorstep waving credentials and looking doctorish. No, she'd shown up in jeans and hiking boots, ogled him from head to toe, and blathered vaguely about helping him with his "problems." It was no wonder he'd thought she'd been coming on to him.

Completely off kilter, she tried to smooth her hair, only to encounter her cap. She fought the urge to tug it off, toss it down, and stomp on it in frustration. She desperately needed a few minutes to regroup, clear her head, and figure out how best to proceed.

They would simply have to start over, she decided swiftly, and she would do all in her power to salvage what she could of the situation. Failure was unacceptable. Elisabeth opened her eyes and met his gaze levelly. "Mr. MacKeltar—"

"Dageus," he corrected.

"Mr. MacKeltar, I am going to walk out that door—"

"Please doona be doin' so, lass—"

"—and knock," she continued firmly. "You're going to wait until I knock this time. Then I'm going to introduce myself and explain why I'm here. You're going to say good morning and offer me a cup of coffee. I'm going to drink the whole thing. Then we're going to start over and pretend none of this ever happened. Got it?"

He added sugar to his coffee and licked a few grains from the spoon. "Aye."

Damn him, but he was *still* trying not to laugh, she realized. Under other circumstances, she, too, might have found it amusing—like, if the horrible ordeal had happened to someone else.

"Okay. Here I go."

Elisabeth stalked out and slammed the door so hard that the frame rattled.

Dageus saw her jump a little bit out on the stoop, as if she'd not meant to slam it *quite* so hard.

Leaning back against the counter, he finally let himself laugh. At her display of temper, which he found promising as it hinted of buried passions scarce restrained. At his absurd assumption. At the pleasure of having a woman in his cottage. At feeling like a man—plain and simple. Had she glanced back in the window he was watching her through, she would have seen the picture of relaxation and composure.

Except that every muscle in his body was tensed to spring.

He suspected that if she ventured out into the yard and looked to be running off, he would be tackling her after all. But he'd give her a few minutes to cool off. By Amergin, he needed them, too.

He also needed a few moments to come up with a plan. Fortunately, he'd thought swiftly enough to deflect her question about why he'd assumed she was there to share his bed. It hadn't been as if he could say, *Because it silences the thirteen demons that inhabit me.* Nay, that wouldn't have worked at all.

He couldn't fathom why Gwen had sent her to talk to him, for Gwen surely knew that no amount of poking about in his mind was going to yield solutions or lay the thirteen to rest. He wondered if Gwen had actually told the lass anything about his problem. He doubted it. Although he'd been in the twenty-first century for only five months, he'd read voraciously and had spent many long hours staring in fascination at television. People from Gwen's time didn't believe in anything they couldn't hold in their hands. Nay, Elisabeth Zanders didn't look to be a woman who would readily put her trust in things such as Druids and curses and stones that opened gates through time.

Whye'er she'd come, she'd not be discovering his secrets. If she caught the merest glimpse of what he truly was, she'd flee his vale and ne'er return. Even in his own century the lasses had been wary of the Keltar Druids. Now he was Keltar Druid, and growing darker by the day.

He snorted. She wanted to poke about in his mind? He'd let her try, if such was necessary to keep her near him. But it would be on his terms, not hers. Terms he would swiftly spell out for her.

There was a connection between them, the likes of which he'd naught felt before. A full-blown mating heat. A tension that could make them fight with each other, or fall on each other in an entirely different manner. He wanted to explore that connection—nay, he *needed* to.

A man facing an inevitable death sentence, he was starved for what life remained for him. For a taste of passion; a heady brief swallow of what might have been.

Was it too much to ask that for a few days—a few wee and harmless days—he might forget about the thirteen and be naught but a man?

7

ELISABETH SIPPED HER COFFEE IN SILENCE. IT WAS GOOD and, perversely, that annoyed her. Dark and strong, topped with cream and a sprinkle of raw sugar and cinnamon. Exactly the way she prepared it for herself. Served in a heavy blue-speckled ceramic cup that held the heat. She'd stayed outside long enough that she'd gotten chilled all over again, and she cupped her fingers around the cup, thinking that she didn't like him taking his coffee the same way she did. It made her feel as if they shared something, and she desperately needed distance from the man.

The kitchen was cozy and intimate, with soft lighting, and cabinets and counters fashioned of honeyed oak that matched the gleaming tables and chairs. The pale stone floor was strewn with woven rugs. Handmade baskets held loaves of crusty breads and bottles of wine, and fired clay jars were labeled with names of spices. It seemed simple for such a man. Even dressed in exercise pants and a T-shirt, there was something powerful and complex about him.

And dangerously attractive. *Playgirl's* Man of the Year had nothing on Dageus MacKeltar, she thought ruefully, not that she made a habit of loitering in Barnes & Noble, hiding the annual issue inside a copy of *Woman's World,* peeking through the pages, or anything like that.

Elisabeth glanced at him when he rose and went to the counter, where he transferred the coffee from the brewing pot into a thermal carafe. When his back was to her, she studied him intently, noticing that his hair, caught at the nape, looked like it was folded under several times before he'd wrapped it in a leather thong. *Wow,* she thought, *it must fall to his waist when it's free.* The image of a sleek fall of black silk against a naked golden back was unsettlingly erotic. Then again, everything about the man was unsettlingly erotic.

Standing a good foot taller than her, which put him near six-four, Dageus MacKeltar couldn't have been further from a classic model of a patient needing therapy. He exuded confidence and control. He moved gracefully in his own skin, and seemed easy with silence. He was in exceptional physical condition and didn't appear to have an insecure bone in his body, not that she'd mind hunting for one—and there she went again, veering straight off the path of professionalism.

Mentally shaking herself, she forced herself to focus, to behave as the Dr. Zanders she planned to be one day. She wished she could already claim the barrier of a title before her name. Better yet, she wished she could claim the experience.

She tugged off her cap and smoothed her plait, absently retucking stray curls where she could. "Mr. MacKeltar—"

"Dageus," he interjected, with a smile over his shoulder.

"And take off your coat, lass. Make yourself comfortable."

No way in hell, Elisabeth thought. She needed to be on her toes. She had to get him to agree to counseling. She'd be damned if she'd come all this way, for the promise of so much money, to fail on her first day because she'd made a few bad assumptions. Forcing a smile, she folded her restless hands beneath the table. "Mr. MacKeltar," she said firmly, "I know we didn't quite get off on the right foot—"

"Seemed a fine foot to me," he murmured, moving back toward the table with the carafe.

"—because you didn't know that Gwen had sent for me," she continued, ignoring his comment. "But now that we've cleared things up, I'd like to—"

"Did Gwen say why she wanted you to see me?" he cut her off. Topping off her coffee, he sat down again, placing the carafe on the table.

So much for controlling the conversation, Elisabeth thought, irritably.

"Well?" he prodded ruthlessly. "Aye or nay, lass?"

"Actually," she hedged, "we were supposed to discuss things when I arrived yesterday, but the Jamesons said she won't be getting out of the hospital for a few days." She frowned then, realizing she might have blundered again. Living in the valley perhaps he'd not yet heard about the accident. "Did you know about Gwen's accident?"

"Aye, I spoke with Drustan on the phone yestreen. He said 'twas some blethering American driving on the wrong side of the road."

"If you kept the stupid sheep off the road, an American might have a chance," she said irritably.

His eyes sparkled with amusement. "Had a wee tussle with a sheep, did you then, lass?"

"A mailbox, while trying to avoid one of the meandering little beasts. Why in the world doesn't anyone build fences around here?" she said, exasperated—by sheep, by a crappy flight the day before, by lack of information, and, most especially, by the stubborn Scotsman who kept taking control of the conversation that she was supposed to be in charge of.

"Spoils the beauty. Besides, we Scots doona like to pen things. 'Tis no' our nature."

Now why doesn't that surprise me? Elisabeth thought dryly, eyeing the man who seemed circumscribed by neither inhibition nor a perfectly healthy sense of shame. She took a sip of much-needed caffeine.

"You have no idea why Gwen asked you to come, do you, lass?"

Loath to admit it, she inclined her head, waiting to see what he might tell her.

"'Tis simple. Gwen has a tendency to meddle in the lives of those she cares for. I'd been feeling a bit gloomy for a time, and she fretted. But 'tis naught to fash yourself o'er."

"You were feeling gloomy?" *Fash?* And what had he said moments ago . . . *yestreen?* The man used dozens of words she'd never heard before. Perhaps all Scots did, she decided. The guidebook she'd devoured last week had cautioned that the higher one went into the Highlands, the more likely one was to encounter a thicker accent, even Gaelic.

"For a brief spell. 'Tis no' uncommon. I'd gone through some changes in my life."

"Recent changes?" she pressed, determined to keep him talking. "Job? Marriage? Are you married?" *Zanders, that isn't the way to go about it, you dip. You know the drill—rephrase the last thing they say as a question.*

"Are you asking after your own interests, lass?"

Elisabeth forced herself to smile pleasantly. He'd deflected her question with a question of his own. The man was not cooperating at all. Nimbly, she redirected. "It helps if I know something about you. I thought we'd start with the basics. Why don't we begin with your age?"

"I've a score and ten or thereabouts," he said easily. "And, nay, I'm no' wed. But tit for tat, lass. How old are you?"

She shook her head.

"What harm is there in answering such a wee question? I'm answering yours. I'm under no obligation to do so," he reminded pointedly. "Nor will I continue if you won't."

A few moments of silence ensued until she said grudgingly, "Twenty-four." It sounded young, even to her. Any minute now he would ask how long she'd been practicing and she'd be forced to admit she was still a student. She may as well stand up and fling what remained of her credibility out the window. She'd already left the bulk of it on his doorstep.

"Are you married?" he asked.

She was so relieved that he'd not pressed the issue of her age and expertise, or lack thereof, that she answered him. "No, I'm not. But, Mr. MacKeltar, you really should let me ask the questions."

"Dageus. Betrothed?"

"That's an old-fashioned word," Elisabeth murmured. She added it to the store of others she was collecting from him.

"I'm an old-fashioned man, lass. So?"

"This isn't about me."

"Well, 'tis no' about me, because I've no need of your services."

"Gwen seemed to think you did."

"I explained that—she frets o'er much."

Elisabeth let the silence unfurl, wondering what he would do with it. He did nothing. He sat perfectly still and composed, staring levelly at her. So for a good two minutes, which felt like ten, they stared at each other. Until she was shocked to discover that she'd folded her arms and crossed her legs.

That he took pity on *her* unsettled her more than anything that had happened so far, and it hadn't exactly been a banner morning.

"What, no more questions?" he asked, his golden eyes glittering.

"Do you have children?" she blurted, hastily unfolding her arms. *Where did that come from, Zanders?* She fought the urge to close her eyes and sink under the table.

"With no *wife*?" he said indignantly. "What manner of man do you take me for? Have you children?" he flung it right back at her.

"No," she said, dismayed to hear herself sound as defensive as he had. She took a deep breath, and bleakly acknowledged that she shouldn't have come back in the cottage the second time. She simply wasn't in top form. It occurred to her that he might not have anywhere near the presence she was attributing to him. Perhaps she was simply so jet-lagged that everything seemed larger than life and insurmountable this morning.

She seized upon the excuse gratefully. If only she'd recognized it sooner, after their initial fiasco of a conversation, she would have coolly and professionally informed him that she'd come back the next day. The sooner she terminated this conversation, the better. God only knew what might come out of her mouth if she stayed. She would retreat, rest, and return the cool, focused Elisabeth Zanders who had earned, and would fight to keep, the highest GPA in the psych department at Harvard.

"I'm sorry, Mr. MacKeltar," she apologized, abruptly pushing her cup away and rising to her feet, "but I'm afraid I'm not quite myself this morning. It's become apparent to me that I'm far more jet-lagged than I'd realized."

"Is that what you'll blame it on, then, lass?" he said softly, standing as well.

His tongue flickered out, wetting his full lips in a gesture that purred invitation, and dared her to acknowledge it. His golden eyes met hers, and for an awful moment Elisabeth felt like he was seeing right into her soul. That he was fully aware of the impact he had on her, and would wait patiently until she admitted it. That the man standing before her could manipulate circles around her. That there wasn't a single psychologist's tactic she could use on him that he wouldn't see right through.

A good psychologist would have said, *Blame* what *on?* and confronted him. But she didn't, because she wasn't entirely certain he wouldn't baldly reply, *The fact that I throw you off balance because you can't stop thinking about getting me naked.*

And she was thinking about it. Every time she looked at him.

"Thank you for the coffee, Mr. MacKeltar," she said smoothly, pretending there was no palpable, mind-boggling tension charging the air between them. She was damned if she was going to request his permission to counsel him, she decided. With such a strong-willed man, it would be far wiser to proceed matter-of-factly. To act as if whether or not she was going to treat him wasn't even in question. "Let's set a time for tomorrow so we can get off to a fresh start," she said firmly.

And tonight she would phone Gwen and pick her brain clean. There was no way she was approaching Dageus Mac-Keltar again until she knew more about him.

"You wouldn't be thinking of troubling Gwen while she's in the hospital, would you now?" Dageus said softly. "With Gwen's delicate condition and the traumatic accident, I'll no' have you upsetting her." Clearly Gwen had some kind of plan involving the lass, Dageus mused, or she wouldn't have hired her, but he didn't think Gwen would tell her about the thirteen, at least not in a casual phone conversation, or she would have already done so. Still, he would take no chances. Elisabeth Zanders was a lovely wee lass with fire and intelligence and, if he was clever, he could have her all to himself for a time. The intensity of his determination to have her, to explore what she thought and felt, to learn the feel of her body yielding naked and warm beneath his, startled him. Were he a man of single-minded clarity, such determination might have done more than startle him, it might have warned him. But he wasn't. And it didn't.

Elisabeth was shocked by how accurately he'd guessed her thoughts. While she floundered for a response, he stepped closer. The man really had a thing for invading personal space.

"Have dinner with me this eve, lass," he purred, plucking

her cap from her hands and gently smoothing it over her hair.

"I'm a fair cook."

She backed up hastily, just as the tips of his fingers brushed her ear. She tingled where he'd touched her. "Tomorrow."

He studied her intently. After a moment, he seemed to decide that she wasn't going to budge an inch on that. "Tomorrow then. Breakfast with me."

"One o'clock," she countered firmly, backing down the hallway toward the door.

"Or forget it," he said flatly, stalking her down the hallway.

She stopped backing when her spine hit the door.

He stopped a foot from her. "The way I see it, Elisabeth Zanders, you've a bit of a problem, doona you?"

When she didn't reply, he smiled. It didn't quite reach his eyes.

"Aye, you do. Gwen asked you to come talk with me. I'll wager she's paying you for your time, is she no'?"

Elisabeth nodded tightly. His golden eyes, unblinking and predatorily patient, reminded her of a tiger's. A shiver kissed her spine.

"I'll wager she's paying you well, seeing as she brought you all the way from America."

Elisabeth gave him a frosty stare. She could see full well where he was going with it and didn't like it one bit.

"'Twould seem I have something you need," he said silkily. "One might even say I *am* something you need." His smile grew, but oddly, so did the chill in his gaze.

Elisabeth gritted her teeth, refused to reply.

He waited in silence.

Finally, she gave him a faint, tight nod.

"Mayhap we should strike a bargain, lass."

"What do you have in mind?" she asked coolly.

"Being that Gwen is dear to me, if she wishes me to see you, then see you I shall. But"—once again, he placed his palms against the door on either side of her head—"'twill be as a guest in my home. If you wish to practice your study of the mind on me, 'twill be on my terms. We'll put Gwen's mind at ease and you'll earn your wages. You'll no' trouble Gwen or Drustan with any questions, nor will you share with them anything we discuss, because the moment you do, 'tis o'er betwixt us. Understand?"

Elisabeth felt as if the breath had been knocked out of her. In a few sentences, he'd fenced her into a tidy little corner, using Gwen's peace of mind and well-being during her pregnancy as his weapon. And she knew he meant every word of it.

She'd already made a mess of things by not waiting for Gwen. If he refused to see her, she'd be in a serious bind. Fifty thousand dollars' worth of a bind. She'd be in the embarrassing position of having to inform Gwen that she couldn't even get in his door. She'd have left school midterm, for nothing. She'd have to go back to Harvard, back to the *Beanpole* for goodness' sake, a failure. Oh, she'd sooner die a virgin tomorrow!

Suddenly it was perfectly clear why Gwen had offered so much money. The man didn't want counseling, didn't think he needed it, was too intelligent by far, and indisputably a master strategist. Simply finding out what his problem was would be a greater challenge than any she'd ever faced. She felt a strange thrill at the thought of getting inside such a man's mind.

Could she? she wondered. The tension between them was thick enough to cut into bricks and build a wall. If she could navigate the labyrinth of his mind, she'd never again suffer doubts about her abilities to counsel. If she could conquer him, she could handle anything.

"Breakfast tomorrow then?" he repeated, leaning into her. His golden eyes held hers in a wordless challenge. "What are you afraid of, lass?" he said softly.

He used physical closeness as a weapon, she realized. He fully intended it to throw her off balance.

Thrusting her chin in the air, she met his gaze levelly. Tomorrow was another day, tomorrow she'd be completely on her toes, up to any challenge. She would accept his terms because she had no alternative, but all the while he would be treating her as his guest, she'd patiently and cleverly probe him as a psychologist.

"Fine. I'll be here at nine," she said smoothly, thinking that the Elisabeth Zanders he would meet tomorrow would be vastly different from the one he'd run ramshod over today. She gave him a pleasant smile, ducked from between his arms, and twisted the doorknob. Naturally the door didn't budge because a good two-hundred-plus pounds were leaning against it. Arching a brow, she gave him an imperious look.

Smiling faintly, he dropped his hands.

She took care to close the door gently behind her.

Dageus watched her from the window until she disappeared over the crest of the hill. For the first time in a long time, the morrow's sunrise seemed to hold promise.

Deep inside, far from defeated, the thirteen stirred restlessly, murmuring approval, and for a change, being of a like mind with the ancient ones didn't fash him in the least. For a moment, he even enjoyed the thirteen's camaraderie, think- ing mayhap he had a thing or two in common with the Tuatha Dé Danann Druids. Though they were separated by millennia, men were men in any day and age.

'Tis for but a few days, he reminded himself. *'Til Gwen and Drustan return.*

He couldn't fathom what Gwen's plan involving the lass was, but he was fair certain tooping wasn't part of it. And when she found out, she'd be furious with him.

He'd deal with that when need be.

In the meantime, he planned to wedge as much life as possible into the next few days.

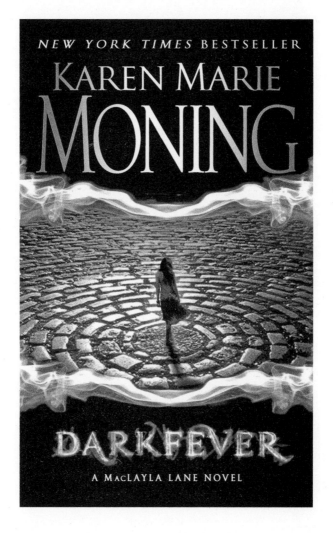

KAREN MARIE
MONING

DARKFEVER

A MacLAYLA LANE NOVEL

DARKFEVER

My name is MacKayla, Mac for short. I'm a sidhe-*seer, a person who can see the Fae, a fact I accepted only recently and very reluctantly.*

My philosophy is pretty simple: Any day nobody's trying to kill me is a good day in my book. I haven't had many good days lately. Not since the walls between Man and Fae came down. But then, there's not a sidhe-*seer alive who's had a good day since then.*

When MacKayla's sister is murdered, she leaves a single clue to her death—a cryptic message on Mac's cell phone. Journeying to Ireland in search of answers, Mac is soon faced with an even greater challenge: staying alive long enough to master a power that she had no idea she possessed—a gift that allows her to see beyond the world of Man, into the dangerous realm of the Fae.

As Mac delves deeper into the mystery of her sister's death, her every move is shadowed by the dark, mysterious Jericho, while at the same time, the ruthless V'lane—an immortal Fae who makes sex an addiction for human women—closes in on her. As the boundary between worlds begins to crumble, Mac's true mission becomes clear: find the elusive *Sinsar Dubh* before someone else claims the all-powerful Dark Book—because whoever gets to it first will have complete control, and nothing less, of both worlds.

1

A YEAR EARLIER...

JULY 9. ASHFORD, GEORGIA. NINETY-FOUR DEGREES, 97 PERcent humidity.

It gets crazy hot in the South in the summer, but it's worth it to have such short, mild winters. I like most all seasons and climes. I can get into an overcast drizzly autumn day—great for curling up with a good book—every bit as much as a cloudless, blue summer sky, but I've never cared much for snow and ice. I don't know how northerners put up with it. Or why. But I guess it's a good thing they do, otherwise they'd all be down here crowding us out.

Native to the sultry southern heat, I was lounging by the pool in the backyard of my parents' house, wearing my favorite pink polka-dotted bikini that went perfectly with my new I'm-not-really-a-waitress-pink manicure and pedicure. I was sprawled in a cushion-topped chaise soaking up the sun, my long, blond hair twisted up in a spiky knot on top of my head in one of those hairdos you really hope nobody ever catches you wearing. Mom and Dad were away on vacation, celebrating their thirtieth wedding anniversary with a twenty-one-day island-hopping cruise through the tropics, which had begun two weeks ago in Maui and ended next weekend in Miami.

I'd been working devotedly on my tan in their absence, taking quick dips in the cool, sparkling blue, then stretching out to let the sun toast drops of water from my skin, wishing my sister Alina was around to hang out with, and maybe invite a few friends over.

My iPod was tucked into my dad's Bose sound dock on the patio table next to me, bopping cheerily through a playlist that I'd put together specifically for poolside sunning, comprised of the top one hundred one-hit wonders from the past few decades, plus a few others that make me smile—happy mindless music to pass happy mindless time. It was currently playing an old Louis Armstrong song—"What a Wonderful World." Born in a generation that thinks cynical and disenchanted is cool, sometimes I'm a little off the beaten track. Oh well.

A tall glass of chilled sweet tea was at hand, and the phone was nearby in case Mom and Dad made ground sooner than expected. They weren't due ashore the next island until tomorrow, but twice now they'd landed sooner than scheduled. Since I'd accidentally dropped my cell phone in the pool a few days ago, I'd been toting the cordless around so I wouldn't miss a call.

Fact was I missed my parents like crazy.

At first, when they left, I'd been elated by the prospect of time alone. I live at home and when my parents are there the house sometimes feels annoyingly like Grand Central Station, with Mom's friends, Dad's golf buddies, and ladies from the church popping in, punctuated by neighborhood kids stopping over with one excuse or another, conveniently clad in their swim trunks—gee, could they be angling for an invitation?

But after two weeks of much longed-for solitude, I'd begun choking on it. The rambling house seemed achingly quiet, especially in the evenings. Around supper time I'd been feeling downright lost. Hungry, too. Mom's an amazing cook and I'd burned out fast on pizza, potato chips, and mac 'n' cheese. I couldn't wait for one of her fried chicken, mashed potatoes, fresh turnip greens, and peach pie with homemade whipped cream dinners. I'd even done the grocery shopping in anticipation, stocking up on everything she needed.

I love to eat. Fortunately, it doesn't show. I'm healthy through the bust and bottom, but slim through the waist and thighs. I have good metabolism, though Mom says, "Ha, wait until you're thirty. Then forty, then fifty." Dad says, "More to love, Rainey," and gives Mom a look that makes me concentrate really hard on something else. Anything else. I adore my parents, but there's such a thing as TMI. *Too much information.*

All in all, I have a great life, short of missing my parents and counting the days until Alina gets home from Ireland, but both of those are temporary, soon to be rectified. My life will go back to being perfect again before much longer.

Is there such a thing as tempting the Fates to slice one of the most important threads that holds your life together simply by being too happy?

When the phone rang, I thought it was my parents.

It wasn't.

It's funny how such a tiny, insignificant, dozen-times-a-day action can become a line of demarcation.

The picking up of a phone. The pressing of an ON button.

Before I pressed it—as far as I knew—my sister was alive. At the moment of pressing, my life split into two distinct epochs: Before the call and After the call.

Before the call, I had no use for a word like *demarcation,* one of those fifty-cent words I knew only because I was an avid reader. Before, I floated through life from one happy moment to the next. Before, I thought I knew everything. I thought I knew who I was, where I fit, and exactly what my future would bring.

Before, I thought I *had* a future.

After the call, I began to discover that I'd never really known anything at all.

I waited two weeks from the day that I learned my sister had been murdered for somebody to do something—anything—besides plant her in the ground after a closed-casket funeral, cover her with roses, and grieve.

Grieving wasn't going to bring her back, and it sure wasn't going to make me feel better knowing that whoever'd killed her was walking around alive out there somewhere, happy in their sick little psychotic way, while my sister lay icy and white beneath six feet of dirt.

Those weeks will remain forever foggy to me. I wept the entire time, vision and memory blurred by tears. My tears were involuntary. My soul was leaking. Alina wasn't just my sister; she was my best friend. She'd emailed incessantly and we'd spoken weekly, sharing everything, keeping no secrets.

Or so I thought. Boy, was I ever wrong.

We'd been planning to get an apartment together when she came home. We'd been planning to move to the city, where I was finally going to get serious about college, and Alina was going to work on her Ph.D. at the same Atlanta university. It was no secret that my sister had gotten all the ambition in the family. Since graduating high school, I'd been perfectly content bartending at The Brickyard four or five nights a week, living at home, saving most of my money, and taking just enough college courses at the local Podunk university (one or two a semester, and classes like How to Use the Internet and Travel Etiquette, which didn't cut it with my folks) to keep Mom and Dad reasonably hopeful that I might one day graduate and get a Real Job in the Real World. Still, ambition or no, I'd been planning to really buckle up and make some big changes in my life when Alina returned.

When I'd said good-bye to her months earlier at the airport, the thought that I wouldn't see her alive again had never crossed my mind. Alina was as certain as the sun rising and setting. She was charmed. She was twenty-four and I was twenty-two. We were going to live forever. Thirty was a million light-years away. Forty wasn't even in the same galaxy. Death? Ha. Death happened to really old people.

Not.

After two weeks, my teary fog started to lift a little. I didn't stop hurting. I think I just finally expelled the last drop of moisture from my body that wasn't absolutely necessary to keep me alive. And rage watered my parched soul. I wanted answers. I wanted justice. I wanted revenge. I seemed to be the only one.

I'd taken a psych course a few years back that said people dealt with death by working their way through stages of grief. I hadn't gotten to wallow in the numbness of denial that's supposed to be the first phase. I'd flashed straight from numb to pain in the space of a heartbeat. With Mom and Dad away, I was the one who'd had to identify her body. It hadn't been pretty and there'd been no way to deny that Alina was dead.

After two weeks, I was thick into the anger phase. Depression was supposed to be next. Then, if one was healthy, acceptance. Already I could see the beginning signs of acceptance in those around me, as if they'd moved directly from numbness to defeat. They talked of "random acts of violence." They spoke about "getting on with life." They said they were "sure things were in good hands with the police."

I was so not healthy. Nor was I remotely sure about the police in Ireland. Accept Alina's death? Never.

"You're *not* going, Mac, and that's final." Mom stood at the kitchen counter, a towel draped over her shoulder, a cheery red, yellow, and white magnolia-printed apron tied at her waist, her hands dusted with flour.

She'd been baking. And cooking. And cleaning. And baking some more. She'd become a veritable Tasmanian devil of domesticity. Born and raised in the Deep South, it was Mom's way of trying to deal. Down here, women nest like mother hens when people die. It's just what they do.

We'd been arguing for the past hour. Last night the Dublin police had called to tell us that they were terribly sorry, but due to a lack of evidence, in light of the fact that they didn't have a single lead or witness, there was nothing left to pursue. They were giving us official notice that they'd had no choice but to turn Alina's case over to the unsolved division, which anyone with half a brain knew wasn't a division at all but a filing cabinet in a dimly lit and largely forgotten basement storeroom somewhere. Despite assurances that they would periodically reexamine the case for new evidence, that they would exercise utmost due diligence, the message was clear: Alina was dead, shipped back to her own country, and no longer their concern. They'd given up.

Was that record time or what? Three weeks. A measly twenty-one days. It was inconceivable!

"You can bet your butt if we lived over there, they'd never have given up so quickly," I said bitterly.

"You don't know that, Mac." Mom pushed her ash-blond bangs back from her blue eyes, red-rimmed from weeping, leaving a smudge of flour on her brow.

"Give me the chance to find out."

Her lips compressed into a thin white-edged line. "Absolutely not. I've already lost one daughter to that country. I will not lose another."

Impasse. And here we'd been ever since breakfast, when I'd announced my decision to take time off so I could go to Dublin and find out what the police had really been doing to solve Alina's murder.

I would demand a copy of the file, and do all in my power to motivate them to continue their investigation. I would give a face and a voice—a loud and hopefully highly persuasive one—to the victim's family. I couldn't shake the belief that if only my sister had a representative in Dublin, the investigation would be taken more seriously.

I'd tried to get Dad to go, but there just wasn't any reaching him right now. He was lost in grief. Though Alina and I had different faces and builds, we had the same color hair and eyes, and the few times Dad had actually looked at me lately, he'd gotten such an awful look on his face that it had made me wish I was invisible. Or brunette with brown eyes like him, instead of sunny blond with green eyes.

Initially, after the funeral, he'd been a dynamo of determined action, making endless phone calls, contacting anyone and everyone. The embassy had been kind, but directed him to Interpol, which had kept him busy for a few days "looking into things" before diplomatically referring him back to where he'd begun—the Dublin police. The Dublin police remained unwavering. No evidence. No leads. Nothing to investigate. *If you have a problem with that, sir, contact your embassy.*

He called the Ashford police—no, they couldn't go to Ireland and look into it. He called the Dublin police again—were they sure they'd interviewed every last one of Alina's friends and fellow students and professors? I hadn't needed to hear both sides of that conversation to know that the Dublin police were getting testy.

He'd finally placed a call to an old college friend who held some high-powered, hush-hush position in the government. Whatever that friend said had deflated Dad completely. He'd closed the door on us and not come out since.

The climate was decidedly grim in the Lane house, with Mom a tornado in the kitchen, and Dad a black hole in the study. I couldn't sit around forever waiting for them to snap out of it. Time was wasting and the trail was growing colder by the minute. If someone was going to do something, it had to be now, which meant it had to be me.

I said, "I'm going and I don't care if you like it or not."

Mom burst into tears. She slapped the dough she'd been

kneading down on the counter and ran out of the room. After
a moment, I heard the bedroom door slam down the hall.

That's one thing I can't handle—my mom's tears. As if
she hadn't been crying enough lately, I'd just made her cry
again. I slunk from the kitchen and crept upstairs, feeling
like the absolute *lowest* of the lowest scum on the face of the
earth.

I got out of my pajamas, showered, dried my hair, and
dressed, then stood at a complete loss for a while, staring
blankly down the hall at Alina's closed bedroom door.

How many thousands of times had we called back and
forth during the day, whispered back and forth during the
night, woken each other up for comfort when we'd had bad
dreams? I was on my own with bad dreams now.

Get a grip, Mac. I shook myself and decided to head up to
campus. If I stayed home, the black hole might get me, too.
Even now I could feel its event horizon expanding exponen-
tially.

On the drive uptown, I recalled that I'd dropped my cell
phone in the pool—God, had it really been all those weeks
ago?—and decided I'd better stop at the mall to get a new
one in case my parents needed to reach me while I was out. *If*
they even noticed that I was gone.

I stopped at the store, bought the cheapest Nokia they
had, got the old one deactivated, and powered up the replace-
ment.

I had fourteen new messages, which was probably a record for me. I'm hardly a social butterfly. I'm not one of those
plugged-in people who are always hooked up to the latest,
greatest find-me service. The idea-messaging capability. I

don't have Internet service or satellite radio, just your basic account, thank you. The only other gadget I need is my trusty iPod—music is my great escape.

I got back in my car, turned on the engine so the air conditioner could do battle with July's relentless heat, and began listening to my messages. Most of them were weeks old, from friends at school, or The Brickyard, who I'd talked to since the funeral.

I guess, somewhere in the back of my mind, I'd made the connection that I'd lost cell service a few days before Alina had died and was hoping I might have a message from her. Hoping she might have called, sounding happy before she died. Hoping she might have said something that would make me forget my grief, if only for a short while. I was desperate to hear her voice just one more time.

When I did, I almost dropped the phone. Her voice burst from the tiny speaker, sounding frantic, terrified.

"Mac! Oh God, Mac, where *are* you? I need to talk to you! It rolled straight into your voice mail! What are you *doing* with your cell phone turned off? You've got to call me the *minute* you get this! I mean, the very instant!"

Despite the oppressive summer heat, I was suddenly icy, my skin clammy.

"Oh, Mac, everything has gone so wrong! I thought I knew what I was doing. I thought he was helping me, but— God, I can't believe I was so stupid! I thought I was in love with him and he's one of them, Mac! He's one of *them*!"

I blinked uncomprehendingly. One of who? For that matter, who was this "he" who was one of "them" in the first place? Alina . . . in love? No way! Alina and I told each other everything. Aside from a few guys she'd dated casually her first months in Dublin, she'd not mentioned any other guy in her life. And certainly not one she was in love with!

Her voice caught on a sob. My hand tightened to a death grip on the phone, as if maybe I could hold on to my sister through it. Keep *this* Alina alive and safe from harm. I got a few seconds of static, then when she spoke again she lowered her voice, as if fearful of being overheard.

"We've got to talk, Mac! There's so much you don't know. My God, you don't even know what you *are*! There are so many things I should have told you, but I thought I could keep you out of it until things were safer for us. I'm going to try to make it home"—she broke off and laughed bitterly, a caustic sound totally unlike Alina—"but I don't think he'll let me out of the country. I'll call you as soon—" More static then a gasp. "Oh, Mac, he's coming!" Her voice dropped to an urgent whisper. "Listen to me! We've got to find the"— her next word sounded garbled or foreign, something like *shi-sadu*, I thought. "Everything depends on it. We can't let them have it! We've *got* to get to it first! He's been lying to me all along. I know what it is now and I know where—"

Dead air. The call had been terminated.

I sat stunned, trying to make sense of what I'd just heard. I thought I must have a split personality and there were two Macs: one that had a clue about what was going on in the world around her, and one that could barely track reality well enough to get dressed in the morning and put her shoes on the right feet. Mac-that-had-a-clue must have died when Alina did, because this Mac obviously didn't know the first thing about her sister.

She'd been in love and never mentioned it to me! Not once. And now it seemed that was the least of the things she'd not told me. I was flabbergasted. I was betrayed. There was a whole, huge part of my sister's life that she'd been withholding from me for *months*.

What kind of danger had she been in? What had she been trying to keep me out of? Until *what* was safer for us? What did we have to find? Had it been the man she'd thought she was in love with that had killed her? Why—oh *why*—hadn't she told me his name?

I checked the date and time on the call—the afternoon after I'd dropped my cell phone in the pool. I felt sick to my stomach. She'd needed me and I hadn't been there for her. At the moment that Alina had been so frantically trying to reach me, I'd been sunning lazily in the backyard, listening to my top one hundred mindless, happy songs, my cell phone lying short-circuited and forgotten on the dining room table.

I carefully pressed the SAVE key then listened to the rest of the messages, hoping she might have called back, but there was nothing else. According to the police, she'd died approximately four hours after she'd tried reaching me, although they hadn't found her body in an alley for nearly two days.

That was a visual I always worked really hard to block.

I closed my eyes and tried not to dwell on the thought that I'd missed my last chance to talk to her, tried not to think that maybe I could have done something to save her if only I'd answered. Those thoughts could make me crazy.

I replayed the message again. What was a *shi-sadu*? And what was the deal with her cryptic, *You don't even know what you are*? What could Alina possibly have meant by that?

By my third run-through, I knew the message by heart.

I also knew that there was no way I could play it for Mom and Dad. Not only would it drive them further off the deep

end (if there *was* a deeper end than the one they were currently off), but they'd probably lock me in my room and
throw away the key. I couldn't see them taking any chances
with their remaining child.

But . . . if I went to Dublin and played it for the police,
they'd have to reopen her case, wouldn't they? This was a
bona fide lead. If Alina had been in love with someone, she
would have been seen with him at some point, somewhere.
At school, at her apartment, at work, somewhere. Somebody
would know who he was.

And if the mystery man wasn't her killer, surely he was
the key to discovering who was. After all, he was "one of
them."

I frowned.

Whoever or whatever *they* were.

ABOUT THE AUTHOR

KAREN MARIE MONING is the *New York Times* bestselling author of the Fever series, featuring MacKayla Lane, and the award-winning Highlander series. She has a bachelor's degree in society and law from Purdue University and is currently working on a new series set in the Fever world and a graphic novel featuring MacKayla Lane.

www.karenmoning.com

About the Type

This book was set in Granjon, a modern recutting of a typeface produced under the direction of George W. Jones, who based Granjon's design upon the letter forms of Claude Garamond (1480–1561). The name was given to the typeface as a tribute to the typographic designer Robert Granjon.

ARE YOU COUNTING DOWN THE
MINUTES UNTIL YOU GET YOUR NEXT FIX
OF THE FEVER WORLD?

———

Turn the page for a sensational sneak peek
at some of the art that will appear in
Mac's graphic novel debut...